TUNE IN TOMORROW

Laura Michaels

A KISMET™ Romance

METEOR PUBLISHING CORPORATION
Bensalem, Pennsylvania

KISMET™ is a trademark of Meteor Publishing Corporation

First Printing March 1992.

ISBN: 1-878702-81-5

Printed in the United States of America

For A.N., J.R. and B.V., always there.

LAURA MICHAELS

Laura Michaels is the pseudonym of a popular romance writer fascinated by small-town life and the characters to be found there. A refugee from the big city, she lives at the end of a New England dirt road, steps over small children to get to her desk, and would rather write than do just about anything except bobsledding.

PROLOGUE

"If Ron Hauster were a character in a book, the book would be a romance and he'd be the hero. For more than a decade, this hard-driving tycoon has dominated the New York business scene. His yacht, his triplex apartment, his fleet of private jets are all legendary, not to mention the beautiful women who compete for his attentions. He's got it all, or at least he used to."

Liz Sherwood paused, took a breath and looked straight into the camera. It was 6:42 P.M. EST on a pleasant Tuesday in April. She was live from Washington, D.C., seven minutes into the network nightly news. Approximately thirty-two million Americans were tuned in, some watching as they ate dinner, others having just gotten home from work and trying to relax while catching up on world events. That they chose to do it with Elizabeth Jane Sherwood was no real surprise. After eight years on camera, she was one of the most trusted and liked women in America (so a recent poll said). She was smart, level-headed, nice to look at and—get this—honest.

"Sometimes, Elizabeth Jane," her mother used to say, "you don't have to tell everything you know. Sometimes it pays to keep things to yourself."

Maybe so back home in Abilene, Texas, but in the dog-eat-dog world of television news, it paid—in spades—to know of what you spoke and speak of it clearly.

"There's only one problem," Elizabeth Jane Sherwood told America. "Ron Hauster is broke."

Ker-boom. As that little bombshell went lobbing out over the heartland, the anchor broke for a commercial, collapsed back in his chair, and groaned.

"You did it," Tom Wilcox said. "You actually did it." He smiled his pretty-boy smile under his blow-dried hair and took a quick sip from the can of diet soda hidden under the anchor desk. "Better you than me, sweetheart."

With Florshine floor polish, you'll never mop again! Smudges, scuffs, and stains all disappear! Florshine, florshine, florshine! For beautiful floors!

The little red light on the camera flashed again.

Tom gave America his sincerely concerned look and did the hand-off back to Liz.

The piece ran three minutes, long by television standards. It detailed Hauster's strategy of borrowing from Peter to pay Paul while creating for himself an extravagantly hyped image that convinced creditors he was a good risk long after he ceased to be. The evidence was solid; it had to be or the story would never have gotten on the air. Liz did the voice-over on visuals describing the rise of Hauster's real-estate empire, including the major office skyscrapers he'd constructed in Washington and elsewhere, and his gambling empire in Baton Rouge. Several reputable financial analysts explained why the declining market and recent recession could leave him severely overextended, but the clincher was one of his own former aides who spoke on conditions of anonymity and gave persuasive testimony about the shaky state of what he called "Hauster's house of cards".

Twenty minutes later, the broadcast wrapped up. Liz detached the microphone from her silk blouse and handed it to the grip. "Thanks," she said.

The man nodded. He stood aside as she moved out from behind the desk and down the two steps that separated the set from the rest of the studio.

Ed Daugherty was waiting for her. He was a tall, fleshy man with a round face, thinning hair, and piercing eyes. At fifty-two, he was a long-term survivor of the corporate wars. For the past year, he'd been producer of the nightly news. Generally speaking, Liz liked him even though his background was in management rather than journalism. He'd been nervous about her going with the story but now he seemed pleased.

"Nice job," he said. "It hung together better than I thought it would."

Since she'd only sweated bullets over the story for the past month, working on it night and day to make sure she had it absolutely dead to rights, Liz let that go.

Daugherty looked at her thoughtfully. "Why don't we grab some dinner?"

Wilcox bobbed down from the set, hands thrust into his trouser pockets, and grinned at them both. "Good idea. I'm starved."

"Not tonight," Daugherty said. "Liz and me need a little one-on-one." He took her arm and steered her toward the door. On an afterthought, he asked, "What did you say that guy's name was, Tom, the new president of Albania?"

"Saususesceau—suresco—Sausho—"

"Yeah, I thought that was it. Sounds like the new caps aren't working out too good."

Wilcox flushed. He'd been away on "assignment" for a couple of weeks having a little tuck here and a little nip there. That was covered in his contract, but he'd decided to go a little further. He'd gotten his caps replaced, downed enough diuretics to lose eight pounds, and had his hair tinted a slightly darker shade of chestnut brown to better reflect the studio lights. Just standard procedure for a guy in his position, but Daugherty still liked to rub his nose in it, if only a little.

"Maybe I shouldn't mention my breast implants," Liz said as they got into the elevator. There was no one else on it otherwise she wouldn't have kidded around, not unless she wanted to see an off-the-cuff one-liner transformed into a tabloid headline shrieking from every supermarket checkout.

Daugherty chuckled. "You're not getting me on that one. Maybe I'm a little rough on Wilcox, but so what? He's pulling down four million bucks a year for reading words off a teleprompter. Meanwhile, the ratings suck rocks, the sponsors are screaming, and the only thing up is my blood pressure. That makes him fair game."

Liz privately agreed, but she still thought going after the anchor was kind of like kicking a puppy. She saved her efforts for bigger game—Hauster, for instance.

They went to Mick's, not exactly an original name for an Irish bar, but it was close enough to the building to be convenient, far enough away from the government office buildings to be desirable, and served good stew. Mick himself, or Himself as he was more commonly known, showed them to a booth in the back. He returned right away with two frosty mugs of the best.

"On the house," he said. The floor rocked. Okay, it didn't but it could have.

"You're kidding," Liz said.

"Yours," Mick clarified, "not his. That was a nice job you did on Hauster."

"Nice *story* I did on Hauster. I didn't do a job on him."

"Wanna bet?" Mick asked. "He put up that damn building down the street, you know that? Had the whole sidewalk torn up for a month. My customers had to climb over it to get in. Did the city care? Of course not. Hauster had everyone and his grandmother on the take. Now he's going down for the count and it couldn't happen to a nicer guy. Got chili tonight, want some?"

"What happened to the stew?" Daugherty demanded. Not getting in on free beer ticked him off.

"Hey, the neighborhood's changing. I gotta diversify. You want some or not?"

Liz nodded. Daugherty pretended to think about it. "I guess, but no onions on mine," he said finally.

Mick went off, the door banged as some more people came in, somewhere in the background a radio played "I Can't Get No Satis-FAAAC-tion". Vintage Stones.

"Someday," Liz said, "we'll be doing a piece on this concert, see. There'll be all these little old people in wheelchairs, and up on the stage there'll be this skinny old man flopping around, waving his arms, singing. Mick Jagger, ninety years old, still the best."

"Yummph," Daugherty said. He was a Sinatra man. "So who's next on your hit list?"

"Whatta you mean? Me? Hit list? Hey, I just do my job." But secretly she was pleased. It was still a man's world and being seen as tough couldn't hurt.

"Mind a suggestion?" Daugherty asked.

Mick brought beer nuts, a wad of paper napkins, and a basket of saltines. " 'Nother round?"

Daugherty nodded. "Sure, why not? Whatta you, out killin' the chilis?"

"That's the problem with this town," Mick said, "everybody in a hurry. You can't rush good chili." He wandered off again.

"Wilcox is vulnerable."

Liz was in the middle of a swallow of beer. She didn't choke on it, but she came close. "You're kidding?"

"No, I'm not. His Q's down."

Q scores, otherwise known as the Holy Grail, were the measure by which likability was rated. All ratings mattered, but the Q score said whether or not people would invite you into their homes.

Since that's what they had to do with a nightly network news anchor, it counted big.

"How come?"

"Who knows? Maybe he feels the heat and he's trying a little too hard. Ever since we moved down here from New York the pressure's been on. People can sense that. They want somebody relaxed, confident, but not too much, friendly. Somebody they can trust. Like you."

"My heart's going pitty-pat."

"Try this," Mick said, putting down two brown plastic bowls full of steaming glob. "Guaranteed to clear out your arteries in no time flat."

"I'm a dead man," Daugherty said as he dug in. The look on his face suggested he didn't mind too much.

The chili wasn't as good as Mick's stew, but it wasn't bad, either. They ate in silence for a few minutes until Daugherty came up for air, belched, and said, "I'm serious."

So was Liz. It was serious business. She put down her spoon and gave him the steely-eyed look she'd been working on since she was twelve. "No woman has ever been named anchor of a network nightly news show. The closest any of us has ever come is designated hitter. We get to sit in the chair when the real anchor's away on the understanding that we don't get too comfy."

"That can change. The time's right and you're the person to do it."

"Tom's not a bad guy. He's got more on the ball than you're giving him credit for. He's done a good job."

"Not good enough, not anymore. We need a change. You give the green light and I'll take it to the big boys. Whatta you say?"

"You had to do this over chili? I've got a cast iron stomach, but there are limits."

"Not if you get the anchor seat. Think of it—with that kind of clout, you can interview anybody you want, get any piece you name on the air, actually make things happen. Not to mention the money."

"I make enough money now." She put a hand over her mouth. "I shouldn't have said that. Forget it."

Daugherty chuckled. "Talk about power. I let this out and Vivian'll kill you. Slowly."

Vivian was Vivian Columbine Sanchez, Liz's agent. She'd started out as a secretary for one of the local television stations, gone on the air doing consumer reports, and then decided her real strength lay in arm-twisting. In a part of the business almost totally dominated by men, she was legend. Get Vivian on your good side and you were made. Get her pissed off and you were done for.

Liz was on her good side, so far at least.

"Talk to Vivian," she said, just the way Vivian had taught her.

Daugherty grunted. "That mean you're interested?"

Liz hesitated. She really didn't want to see Tom Wilcox get hurt, but that wouldn't be her decision. If the "big boys" decided to axe him, he was history. He'd get the payoff on his fat contract and the traditional ride into the sunset. All in all, not bad for reading from a teleprompter.

There was a mirror on the wall facing her. She could see herself in it over Daugherty's shoulder. The light was falling across her dark-blond hair and along the curve of her cheek. Unlike Tom, she hadn't been nipped and tucked. There were a few little lines around her blue eyes, but she figured she'd earned them. She was thirty years old, never married, no kids, no pets, not much of anything except work. She was committed to being a good reporter. That really mattered with her. Like it or not, most people got their news from television. A network anchor had tremendous influence on how they perceived the world. She'd be young for the job, but she'd do it honestly. She knew that as sure as she knew anything.

Softly, she said, "I wouldn't say no."

Daugherty grunted. He looked at her for a long moment before he went back to his chili.

Several hundred miles and a world away from Mick's, Ron Hauster sat on the second floor of his triplex apartment above Fifth Avenue. He was in the library, a room that looked like it had been lifted intact out of an English manor house. That was because it had been. He'd bought the manor five years before, disassembled it, and sold the interiors off one by one mostly to Arab and Japanese clients who regarded them as exotic trophies of a world changing rapidly in their favor.

The library he kept for himself. It went nicely in the ultra-modern, sixty-story condominium complex he'd built on the site of an old church. The church dated back to colonial times and included a graveyard, which was why it went for a song because there were still enough squeamish wimps out there to make the market slim. Not Hauster. He went public, talking about the historical significance of the place, the tremendous honor and humility he felt at acquiring it, and his determination to relocate all "the original residents," as he called them, with the same care and reverence he would show his own family.

He bought a bunch of plots in a cemetery upstate and made a big show of transporting the remains with all appropriate ceremony. In fact, the shiny mahogany boxes were empty. Anybody who had been buried in the colonial cemetery was still there, somewhere under the ground floor atrium that housed the condo's health club and restaurant. It was Hauster's little secret and he got a real laugh out of it. He figured he was doing the stiffs a favor letting them get close to the good life even if they'd had to wait a few hundred years to do it. He was that kind of guy.

At the moment, he was dressed in evening clothes impeccably tailored by the same people who did Prince Charles. His shoes alone had cost a grand. Forget the suit, he couldn't even remember what he shelled out for that. Not that it mattered. What counted was looking good, projecting the right image, giving the people what they were dying to pay for. He was a master as it, if he did say so himself, which he did anytime he got the chance because that, too, was good for business. And make no mistake about it, business was all that mattered, nothing else. Not his Barbie-doll wife, not the succession of girlfriends or the sycophants—good word that, he'd learned it a few months ago—who flocked around him. He lived for the deal. When he was doing business, he was in control, making it happen, alive. He was the best.

Which was the reason—the *only* reason—that bitch Sherwood was after him. If he hadn't been the best, she'd never have bothered. You had to give her points for good taste, but that was it. After that, she got nothing. Nothing, nada, nothing, except for grief. That she got in endless supply, the little bitch.

Broke. She'd said he was broke. She looked straight at him through the television screen, straight at the world, and said, "Ron Hauster is broke."

She'd pay for that, oh, boy, would she pay. He got up and walked over to the wall of windows overlooking the street. It never failed to give him a rush, staring down at all the little people running around, waving frantically for taxis that didn't stop or, worse yet, darting into the subway. He went by limo, first class all the way. Never mind that he still looked like what he was, a tough street punk from Brooklyn with a pugnacious nose, little eyes, and a tight, mean mouth. He was the best and God help anybody who forgot it.

He stood there for a few minutes, looking at the street. It was starting to rain. The people down there were getting wet. Rain fell on the glass roof of the atrium and trickled down its sides onto the pavement. There were cracks in the cement. Screwy city, couldn't even do that right.

He turned away from the window and reached for the telephone on top of his desk. The number he punched in was a storefront in Brooklyn, in the old neighborhood where he'd been careful to keep good relations. *You scratch my back, I scratch yours.* The guys he knew understood that. He spoke for five minutes. When he was done, he felt a lot better. Liz Sherwood wanted to play hardball? Fine. He'd give her a game she'd never forget.

*   *   *

At the same time all this was happening, and seemingly unrelated to it, a lamb was being born in a barn in Virginia. Ordinarily, that wasn't a big deal, but this particular lamb was having a hard time of it. It was breached, and its mother, a sweet-tempered ewe named Sheila, was new at the job. This was her first. She wasn't quite sure what to do.

Fortunately, Deke Adler had more experience. He had to since he'd been raising sheep for five years and had gotten so he could tell what one of them was thinking from a hundred yards off. Try telling him they didn't think—in fact, couldn't— and he'd just shrug and say you could believe what you wanted but he had to live with the critters and he knew better.

So the lamb was in trouble and Deke was struggling to help it. Sheila cooperated as best she could. Round about ten P.M. the lamb finally popped free and slid into the world, blinking its eyes and looking as though it had liked it fine where it was. Deke got it cleaned up, made sure Sheila was nursing okay, and went back to the house. He had a shower and thought about fixing himself a decent meal, but he was bone-tired and the effort didn't seem worthwhile. He got a box of cereal from the cupboard, poured some into a salad bowl (the big, mixing kind, because he stood six feet two inches and weighed in at a hundred and ninety pounds of mostly muscle), added milk and sprinkled on a helping of wheat germ at the last second because he did—sometimes—try to be good.

He plopped down in front of the TV, switched it on with the remote, and settled back to watch. The local news was on. This was the news out of Branford, which was the largest town near Woodsley. Woodsley had a population of maybe eight hundred, not counting sheep. Branford boasted five thousand, a little light industry, and some pretty inns that drew the tourists. It also had a middling good TV station that Deke liked to check out from time to time because it was his nearest competition.

Not that his own station, WWDY, could really be compared to the Branford operation. WWDY was a low density transmitter, which meant it could reach just about as far as the nearest ramp on the highway and that was it. On a good day when the solar flares were blowing right, maybe three thousand folks could tune in to WWDY should they choose to do so. It was Deke's hobby; it must have been since he sure wasn't making money from it. Just before signing off to take care of Sheila, he'd gone to automatic with a Bette Davis film festival he was planning to watch himself. But first he thought he'd see what the world had been up to in the intervening hours.

Sam Wheeler was reading the copy. The Branford station was as far as Sam would ever go and that was okay by him. His delivery was calm and well paced.

"Network correspondent Liz Sherwood reported earlier this evening that the financial empire of tycoon Ron Hauster may be on a very shaky foundation. Over expansion and excessive debt could be proving too much for the boy billionaire. A spokesperson for Hauster Industries said there would be no comment on the report at this time. And now the weather."

Hauster, huh? Well, why not? He'd been a symbol of the 1980's, along with little green bottles of mineral water, sun-dried tomatoes, and spiffy foreign cars meant to do 150 mph in the shade. The decade was over, thank God, and Deke didn't miss it. He liked things just fine the way they were now.

Liz Sherwood was that cool blonde with the nice smile. She must have guts, too, to go head-to-head with Hauster. Good for her. He flipped the remote again. Sam Wheeler disappeared, replaced by Bette Davis. Now there was a gutsy lady. Deke settled back to enjoy her, but the day had taken its toll and ten minutes later he was asleep on the couch.

He slept the sleep of honest labor while Liz Sherwood tossed in her solitary bed, thinking about what it would mean to be anchor. Woodsley, Virginia, lay wrapped in slumber while New York rumbled and snorted on the way it always did. In the midst of it, high in his steel-and-glass tower, Ron Hauster slipped a sapphire bracelet on the wrist of his latest mistress and gave himself up to her thanks. She was spared the knowledge that her efforts little touched him, for his mind was elsewhere, wandering the fertile fields of revenge.

ONE

"The problem," one of the Big Boys was saying, "is that the charges made against Mr. Hauster are extremely serious. I stress that 'extremely'. The question has to be asked as to the wisdom of going with such a story without consultation with upper level management and without perhaps ascertaining beyond question the legitimacy of the charges."

His name was Hamilton Wheaton, who was thirty-two years old, a graduate of the Harvard Business School, and currently executive director of corporate affairs for the parent company that owned the network. He was also, in the opinion of Ed Daugherty, a royal pain in the butt.

"Liz Sherwood did a damn good job on this story," Daugherty said. "She did her homework, nailed it down, and went on the air with solid evidence. As for consulting you on a day-to-day program decision, we both know that isn't network policy. That's what they've got me for. Anyway, what I really came by for today was to talk with you about Wilcox. His contract's gonna be up in another—''

Wheaton raised a hand, forestalling him. ''You seem to think this matter with Sherwood is minor, but in fact it is not. I've been on the phone since yesterday evening with members of the board. Everyone is most concerned about Hauster's reaction. *Most* concerned.''

''He's gonna be real pissed,'' Daugherty said. ''That's no mystery. What did you think, he'd be jumping for joy to have everybody find out he's busted? Come on, Wheaton, we had a hell of a story and we went with it. That's how we build ratings, in case you didn't know.''

''Was Mr. Hauster offered the opportunity for a rebuttal?''

''Of course he was. Liz spent a good two weeks trying to run him to earth. He wouldn't return her calls or even comment through a member of his staff. He had his chance and he blew it. If he's unhappy now, it's his own damn fault.''

''That isn't what Mr. Hauster says,'' Wheaton replied. ''He informed the chairman of the board of directors by letter this morning that he regards himself as the victim of a slur campaign, that we aired misrepresentations that will do him grievous financial harm and that he is preparing a major lawsuit against this network.''

"Let him," Daugherty said. "It's his own neck. Liz has got him dead to rights."

Wheaton stood up, smoothed the vents of his hand-made Italian suit, and sighed. "I hope you're not mistaken, for all our sakes. Ron Hauster is a formidable enemy.''

"Ron Hauster is a deadbeat.''

"Maybe so, maybe no. Tell Miss Sherwood I want her here at two P.M. prepared to defend her actions. I want to see the evidence she used to come to her conclusions—all of it. Got that?''

"This isn't how we treat one of our top correspondents, Wheaton.''

"It is when she does something of this magnitude. Just tell her to be here and you come, too.''

"So that's the deal," Daugherty said a short time later. He was sitting in Liz's office, jacket off, brow furrowed, drumming his fingers on the edge of her visitor's chair. "It stinks, but whatta you gonna do? Let's just go, show him what you got, and be done with it. Okay?''

"Fine by me," Liz said. "I can't say I like it, but if that's how he feels, he's welcome to wade through the stuff.''

Daugherty looked relieved. "I appreciate your taking this attitude. It just goes to show what I said yesterday, that you're ready to be anchor.

You keep cool under fire, roll with the punches, and stand by your work. That counts.''

"I hope Wheaton agrees. I don't mind cooperating, but I don't want this to drag on. It's cut and dried as far as I'm concerned.''

"Good, then there won't be any problem. You need any help getting the stuff organized?''

Liz shook her head. "My files are always up to date.'' She smiled at his surprise. The chaos on her desk did not suggest tremendous discipline in that area. "It's self-defense. Come by a few minutes before two in the afternoon. If you want and help me carry the stuff. I'll have a couple of cartons.''

Daugherty whistled under his breath. "That much?''

"You bet. Ham Wheaton's about to regret asking for substantiation. If he wants, I can bury him in it.''

"Great! I knew you'd come through. Okay, I'll see you then.''

He bounced out of the office looking a whole lot more chipper than he had when he came in. Liz stared at the door for a few moments before deciding she'd better get down to work. If she was going to be ready by two, she needed to hustle.

At 1:40, Liz dropped the last file in the cardboard box and glanced at her watch. She had time for a quick pit stop before the meeting with Wheaton. The ladies' room was directly down the hall from her office. She spent maybe five minutes there. Nobody else was around. On such a pleasant spring day, one of the first of the season, everybody had decided to have lunch outside, or at least go for a walk. She returned to her office past the empty desks of the secretaries and other empty offices. It was peaceful for a change, the phones silent, the faxes stilled. In another few minutes, the usual routine would start up again, but the respite gave her a chance to catch her breath.

She heard a door click and vaguely recognized the sound as coming from the stairwell, but her thoughts were elsewhere—on the upcoming meeting. She went back into her office, sat down, and began assembling her thoughts. The smart thing would be to take Wheaton through the story chronologically, from the first tip she'd received to the final coming together of her conclusions. Naturally, she wouldn't name her sources, especially not the all-important Hauster employee. But she'd make clear they were solid. As for the files, he could dissect them as much as he wanted. They left no doubt the story was absolutely accurate. They—

The files were gone. The two cardboard cartons holding them had vanished.

Liz jumped up. She turned around in every direction, looking frantically. No sign of them. She ran out into the open area beyond her office and searched there.

She'd heard the fire door shut. But that was minutes before, and by the time she reached it, there was no sign of anyone in the stairwell. Only deadly, ominous silence reigned until off in the distance she heard the soft whirr of the elevator and a short time later, Ed Daugherty calling her name.

"Liz, you here?"

She was, but the files weren't. They were gone, vanished, vamoosed. She had to go back in there and tell Daugherty her case against Hauster had just walked out the door unless her witnesses came forward again.

Ten hours later—exhausted, depressed, and with the worst headache she'd ever had in her life— Liz finally admitted that wasn't going to happen. The financial analysts who had confirmed her conclusions were suddenly unavailable. Several were described as being "on leave" while the one she'd actually been able to reach sounded panic-stricken and ended up screaming at her never to call him again. As for the former Hauster employee who had insisted on anonymity, he might as well never have existed so completely did he appear to have dropped out of sight.

She sat alone in her office staring out the window at the night-draped city and tried to come to terms with what was happening. She'd done her job intelligently, honestly, and with courage. She'd gotten Hauster dead to rights. In fairness, the network should stand behind her. In reality, there was about as much chance of that as a snowball had on an average day back home in Abilene.

Thirty years old, no husband, no kids, no pets, and—just to top everything off—no job. Elizabeth Jane Sherwood could be pardoned for feeling just a touch sorry for herself. She found a tissue in her desk, blew her nose soundly, and got down to the business of figuring out what to do with the rest of her life.

On a scale of one to ten, we can say that Liz's day was down around zero. On the other hand, back in Woodsley, Virginia, things were looking better. For starters, Sheila and her lamb were doing great. When Deke checked on them again just before dawn, the baby was suckling fine and Sheila looked really proud of herself. So far, so good.

To top everything off, Deke's truck started up the first time he turned the key without any of the coughing and complaining it usually did. Threats to junk it seemed to be working. He rolled the window down, turned his face to the sun, and headed on down the road to Woodsley proper.

We need to clarify something here. Woodsley and proper don't really go together that well. All it means is the center of town, such as it is. Woodsley was founded by the Woodsley clan—they were too numerous even back around 1650 to be called a family—after they bailed out of the Massachusetts Bay Colony because they couldn't, absolutely couldn't, stand those damn Puritans another minute. Whose business was it anyway who went to bed with whom, or who drank what, or whether a body felt stirred to go to church of a Sunday? Nobody's, that's whose.

Thus came Woodsley, founded on a holler, a punch, and a wink. And thus it stayed, retaining down through the centuries a healthy interest in living life to the fullest. All of which sounds great except it tended to spawn a bit too healthy of an interest in a fine, strapping young man of Deke Adler's eminence. He'd gotten pretty good at dodging all the good intentions flung his way, but even he slipped up once in a while. Like now.

He saw Agnes Woodsley coming, he really did. But he was in the middle of paying for a week's worth of groceries so he was stuck. She barreled down on him with all the finesse of an old battleship nobody's got the nerve to junk.

"Deke Adler, as I live and breathe, you get more good-looking every time I see you."

Behind the counter of the Pic & Save Grocery where she was ringing up his purchases, Debbie Woodsley Wiggins just about collapsed. Her cheeks puffed out scarlet and her eyes starting blinking something fierce.

"Aunt Agnes, how could you say that!" she demanded.

"It's just the truth, child, and don't you go pretending you don't know it. There's no room in this world for shrinking violets. Where you been keeping yourself, Deke?"

"Just the usual, Agnes," he said. His strategy in such situations was to be as bland as possible in the hope of deflecting enthusiasm for whatever it was she had in mind this time around. It could be anything from getting his help on one of the endless committees various Woodsleys were always setting up to taking out one of the seemingly thousands of Woodsley female relatives who kept wandering through town on their way who-knew-where.

In this case, it turned out to be the latter.

"My cousin Martha's girl," Agnes said as she followed him out to the truck. "She just finished up at Berkeley and she's coming by for a little visit. Got a real head on her shoulders and pretty to boot. Whatta you say?"

It wasn't easy saying no to a woman who (a) outweighed him by twenty or thirty pounds and (b) was reigning arm-wrestling champion at the ladies' auxiliary. But he did it anyway.

Agnes sighed. She patted her short red hair (most of the Woodsleys were redheads) back into place, hitched up her chinos, and said, "Your loss, but you're gonna change your mind one of these days. Being alone can make a man go all squirrelly, and then who knows what he'll do?

Sure hate to hear you'd blown your brains out or something.''

Deke assured her he had no intention of doing that or anything else like it and got back into the truck. He felt a twinge of guilt at not being more courteous, but he'd learned from experience that you couldn't give most Woodsleys an inch without having them take a mile. That was how they'd gotten the place to start with as any of the original Indian residents could have told you if there had been any still around, which the Woodsleys had long ago seen to that there weren't.

When he got home, he put the groceries away before buckling down to work. His work varied depending on the time of year, but on this particular day he fed the sheep, milked those who hadn't bred that season, and got the churner going to transform the milk into the thick, creamy essence of the cheese he made. With luck, he could turn out several hundred pounds a year which provided a sizable amount of his farm's income. Much more of it came from the five hundred apple trees in his orchards. Later that day, when he had a chance, he needed to check on them.

Toward noon, he threw together a quick sandwich and headed a couple of miles down the road to the WWDY station house. At the strike of noon, he went on the air with the news, some of it culled from the wires and some from messages people had left on his answering machine.

Shelley Woodsley McGiver had given birth to her third child the previous day. Congratulations, Shelley.

Garner Wiggins Woodsley was still laid up from that broken leg. Hope he feels better soon.

In New York, the stock market was down fifteen points on continued rumors of the possible bankruptcy of Ron Hauster. You'd think most folks in Woodsley wouldn't care what the market did, but in fact a lot of them had sizable nest eggs socked away in this and that and they liked to keep up.

And so it went for the fifteen minutes or so it took to cover what was going on in the world. That done, he ran a couple of commercials to pay the bills and went to auto with a selection of Andy Griffith reruns. They were proving unexpectedly popular. Deke didn't know what his ratings were since he couldn't afford to subscribe to any of the services that bothered with such things, but he'd had a sense lately that more people were watching because he was selling more ad time and getting more comments. If that kept up, WWDY might actually end the year in the black for a change.

He spent the afternoon chopping wood, mulching a quarter acre for the vegetable patch he was putting in, and checking on the sheep, plus getting down to the orchard long enough to decide he might be looking at a fair crop. He did the news again at six P.M. and headed home for dinner.

WWDY went off the air at eleven P.M. Some nights Deke threw in an extra news broadcast right before then, sometimes he skipped it, figuring hardly anyone was still awake. On this particular night, he decided he wasn't tired enough to get right to sleep. (No, the day he'd put in hadn't worn him out; he was used to it.)

He was settling down to read the headlines when a particular item on the wire caught his eye. The network was refuting the earlier story on Hauster, saying it was under investigation. He frowned. That didn't look good for Liz Sherwood. He thought about her for a second, remembering how she managed to look friendly and approachable even though she was flat-out gorgeous. Not too many women could pull that off.

She popped back into his mind again as he was driving home through the darkness. Too bad about the Hauster thing, for it could ruin her. But that was the way of the world outside of places like Woodsley. Which was part of why he chose to live as he did, preferring to actually build something rather than spin his wheels on the slippery slopes of ambition.

Not that there weren't drawbacks. Standing under the shower, letting the warm water wash away the stiffness of the day, he wondered if maybe he shouldn't have taken Agnes Woodsley up on her offer. She was right about one thing, that it wasn't good to be alone too much. But he was thirty-two years old, not exactly a kid, and he'd had it with the dating game. He wanted a real, honest-to-God woman who wasn't afraid of commitment, a few kids, and a life built together. In other words, the whole nine yards. Sure he could have settled for less, but he was too stubborn to do it.

"Sometimes," his late father had told him, "you have to settle for what you can get, not what you want." Those had seemed like funny words coming from a guy who was one of the most successful lawyers in Boston, a partner before he was forty, and a millionaire several times over by the time he ended it all going over a cliff with his nineteen-year-old girlfriend in the seat beside him. But the message had been clear enough. Deke's father and mother had endured one of those cold war marriages that went on way too long and finally ended in a dog-fight divorce. Deke had promised himself he'd do better.

He got out of the shower, toweled himself dry, and crawled into bed naked as he always did except in the depths of winter when he wore cotton fleece nightshirts. On this night, a sheet and a light blanket were ample cover. He drifted off, thinking about what he needed to do the next day.

Around one in the morning he woke suddenly with the strange impression that he'd been dreaming about Liz Sherwood. Funny how the mind worked. He didn't know the lady and he sure wasn't likely to. All the same, it took him a while to fall back asleep. He had time to remember that she had cornflower-blue eyes.

Later he'd remember that and shake his head over it, thinking it odd the things he noticed. By then it would be several days later, Liz Sherwood would have been formally "terminated" by the network, and the word would be going around town that Ruth Ann Woodsley Wheaton, the local real-estate maven, remembered selling her a house several years back not three miles outside of Woodsley itself. Imagine that.

"Such a nice woman," Ruth Ann said as she held court at the Colony Diner right across the street from the Pic & Save. This news about the defrocked TV newswoman's connection to Woodsley was the most exciting piece of information to hit the place since Arnold Woodsley Foxxworth admitted being married to two women at the same time and they both said they didn't mind. Quite a guy, old Arnie.

"Not at all up on herself like she might have been," Ruth Ann went on, "considering the money she was making. Said she wanted a little weekend place to get away from it all, but don't you know she's hardly been here since and always kept to herself when she did come. I wonder if she'll want to sell it now."

She spun around on the red leatherette stool, waved so long, and rushed off to get an appraisal put together. She was still typing it out hunt-and-peck on the old Underwood when a spiffy Jaguar purred through town, hung a left on Main Street, and finally came to a stop three miles out in front of the little house Ruth Ann was plotting to unload.

Elizabeth Jane Sherwood got out of the car and looked at the house. The paint was peeling, the porch stairs sagged, and she'd thought it was bigger. Not that any of that mattered. She was in the one place she could still stand to be—the back of beyond—and she was damned well going to stay.

She lugged her suitcase up the walk, fumbled for her key, got the door unlocked, and took two steps inside. Then she screamed.

TWO

"It's only a little bat," Deke said. "It can't hurt you. If it hadn't been disturbed all of a sudden, it wouldn't have tried to get out."

"I'm so sorry," Liz muttered. "How thoughtless of me to walk into my own house. What was it doing in here anyway?"

"Nesting," Deke said. He looked at her carefully, wondering if she was done screaming. She'd been really upset. He'd heard her all the way back down on the road where he was driving by in the truck and had decided he'd better investigate because it sounded for sure as if somebody was getting taken apart with a chain saw.

Instead, it was just one small fruit bat, the same kind that hung out around his apple trees. That and Liz Sherwood herself, cornflower-blue eyes and all, looking not the least bit warm and friendly the way she did on television.

Fact was, she looked pretty damned mad.

"So," he said, "you're here."

She stared at him, looking him up and down, while she debated what to say. Now ordinarily Elizabeth Jane was a nice person; her parents had drummed enough manners into her when she was a kid that she could hold her own pretty much anywhere from Buckingham Palace to the local roller rink—and had. But just then she wasn't feeling any too charitable, especially not to men. She was tired and dirty from the haul out of Washington and the long car ride. Add to that a definite sense of being emotionally battered that came from her final run-in with airhead Wheaton and even worse, her meeting with Ed Daugherty, who was so busy doing the fastest back-pedal in the history of corporate politics that he hardly had time to say good-bye. Let's not even mention Tom Wilcox who came looking for her just as she was finishing packing and who stood there in the hallway with both her hands in his and told her how very, very sorry he was and how she was too good a newswoman to be treated like this. Wilcox, for all the nips, tucks, and diuretics, was a decent man and she'd been willing to see him shafted to get his job. Instead, she was the shaftee. Maybe it was just as well.

"So I'm here," she said finally when she was

done looking at him. "What did you say your name was?"

He'd introduced himself right after scooping the bat up and tossing it through the nearest open window where it took off like the typical bat out of you-know-where and never looked back. Liz prided herself on being able to remember any name, any-time, anywhere, but she'd forgotten his. Less than an hour in the backwoods of Virginia and already her brain was turning to mush. Mind you, it had nothing to do with confronting six-foot-plus of muscled masculinity topped off by a face that was not merely ruggedly handsome but nice to boot. Nothing at all.

"Deke Adler," he said, and held out his hand. It was big, hard, and rough, but the touch was surprisingly gentle. "I own the farm down the road."

Oh, good, he was a neighbor. Just what she needed. Here she was feeling more vulnerable than ever in her entire life and who wanders by, Mr. Knight in Shining Armor. Shining chinos anyway, they looked like he'd had them for a while. So did the frayed around the collar plaid shirt and the scuffed workboots. He really was a farmer, if the mud on those boots was anything to go by, also the calluses on his hand, the weathered texture of his skin, and that all-pervasive air of steadiness that was going straight through her like a hot knife through butter.

Easy on, girl. He was only a man. She was Liz Sherwood, the woman who nailed Yasir Arafat to the wall in the interview where he finally admitted his desperate addiction to kosher hot dogs and pastrami. The same Liz Sherwood who had told Wheaton what he could do with his threat to sue her posterior off for "upsetting Mr. Hauster". The Liz Sherwood who was going to make a new life for herself in this backwoods hole in the wall on her own with no help from anyone. Least of all the big guy bat-catcher from down the road.

"Thanks," she said, reaching for the door. "I appreciate your help, but I don't want to keep you and I have a lot of unpacking to do."

"Okay," Deke said. That was fine with him. Let her find out on her own that bats rarely if ever nested alone. He had better things to do than baby-sit.

So how come when he had one foot out the door he stopped for a second and said, "If you need anything, call me. I'm in the book."

He didn't want her calling him, for God's sake. Let her take care of the bats and everything else on her own just like she obviously wanted to. Still, she did have this hurt look around the eyes which was understandable enough considering what had happened to her but which bothered him all the same. He'd always been a sucker for that kind of thing.

"Thanks," she said, surprised. He sounded as

though he meant it. Naturally, that made her suspicious. She hadn't spent all those years in dog-eat-dog Washington to turn around and let somebody *help* her.

He gave her a last quick up and down before he climbed back into the truck. It sputtered, shot out a stream of exhaust, and finally turned over. When he was gone back down the road, she took a deep breath. The house sat there, empty—she hoped—and not especially inviting.

She lugged her two suitcases inside, dumped them in the front hall, and went exploring. When she bought the house five years before, she'd had some idea about coming down for occasional weekends, rusticating in the country, recharging, that sort of thing. She'd envisioned herself tooling along back lanes hunting for antiques, breathing clean air for a change, and doing whatever else it was people did in such places. None of that had come to pass. The pace of her life hadn't allowed it. The house had simply sat, half forgotten and, it seemed, forlorn.

For a start, it needed a cleaning. There was dust everywhere (where exactly does dust come from in a place with no smog and no grime?), the wallpaper was peeling, the floors were buckling in places, the windows were filthy, and . . . and . . . and . . .

She stood in the center of what she supposed was the living room and shook her head. *How* much had she paid for the place? Of course, that had been back in the eighties when the whole country was nuts. Now it was the sane and sober nineties, and the piper had to be paid.

Cleaning materials to start with and food, she'd need that, too. If memory served, there was a general store in town. It would take work and lots of it to get the place in anything resembling decent shape, but that was exactly what she needed. Good muscle-straining honest work that would send her to bed at night without thoughts or dreams.

There was a bed, wasn't there? She'd furnished the place partially, thinking she'd add more later. Yes, one bed complete with yellowing linens. She wrinkled her nose and added a mental note to get a washer and dryer pronto. If she was staying— and she couldn't think of any reason not to since the rest of the world had definitely lost its appeal—then she might as well be comfortable.

The refrigerator came on the moment she flipped the switch, something to be grateful for. She waited a second to make sure the whir of the motor didn't suddenly stop. For the first time it occurred to her that she'd never heard a refrigerator before. At home in Abilene there had always been too much going on to notice. In Washington, you were lucky if you could hear anything above the drone of the city.

Okay, the refrigerator worked. *And* there was water. A little rusty maybe, but it cleared after a while. That settled it, she was definitely staying. Liz was a list maker, had been all her life. At the moment she was operating from a short one. It had a single item on it: survive. Doggedly, she went about the business of doing just that.

Down at the Pic & Save they were just getting ready to close up. Debbie Woodsley Wiggins was looking forward to getting home so she could get ready for a date with Dan Stimson Woodsley who had been quarterback of the high school football team until he graduated three years before and who was still the best thing she'd ever seen except maybe Tom Selleck and that Deke Adler who just about made her toes curl. Dan didn't do that, but he wasn't bad, either, so she was eager to get the last few customers checked out and get going.

That's when she saw her, the blonde in the gray slacks, white silk blouse, and suede jacket giving the fish eye to the tabloids stacked up next to the counter like she expected one of them to bite her or something.

Oh, my gosh, it really was her. Liz Sherwood, the TV woman, the one who had gotten fired for saying those things about Ron Hauster who, while he wasn't exactly handsome, had this something about him that must come from having all that money.

Ruth Ann had been on the level after all.

"Hi, Miss Sherwood," Debbie said, her voice

kind of breathless what with the excitement of meeting someone who had actually been on Television.

"Hi," Liz said. She might as well start getting used to that. People in Abilene said "hi" all the time and it looked like they did here, too. As far as the girl knowing who she was, that was par for the course. Television made people feel like you were related to them somehow, a second cousin maybe.

"It's really nice to meet you," Debbie said and meant it. Wait'll she told Dan. He never watched the news except for the sports, but he'd know who Liz Sherwood was and you could bet he'd be impressed, maybe even more than he was the time he met that guy from the Miami Dolphins and got so excited.

"Thank you," Liz said. She thought the girl looked vaguely familiar, but then she'd had that impression about most of the people she'd seen as she drove into town.

"I'm Debbie Wiggins," the girl said. She had long red hair pulled back in a ponytail, bright blue eyes, and a pretty smile.

Liz smiled back. "I'm Liz Sherwood," she said because she always did even when someone obviously already knew.

Debbie giggled. "Oh, I know that! We saw you on TV all the time. Just imagine, you coming here to Woodsley. It's so exciting."

Her enthusiasm caught Liz off guard. She wasn't sure what she could say or do that wouldn't automatically be a let down. Whatever else she was at the moment, exciting definitely wasn't it.

So naturally she slipped into interview mode. It had worked for her ever since she was a shy, gawky kid who had trouble making friends and it still did.

"Uh, thanks. Have you worked here long?"

"Two years," Debbie said. "Ever since I got out of school. It's kind of interesting, you know? I mean, not as interesting as what you did—do—uh . . ."

"That's all right," Liz said quietly. It was just as well to have it out in the open. "What I'm doing these days is settling into Woodsley. This is such a pretty place."

No lie there, Woodsley was flat out gorgeous. Unlike other towns in Virginia, it had never been overbuilt. There had been no clear cutting of the magnificent stands of oak, birch, and beech, and no quarrying. Except for the farms and a few winding roads, most of them still dirt, the place looked much as it had when the first Woodsleys discovered it. Over the years, numerous small farms were carved out, but more recently some of them had been abandoned as some of the younger folks moved on. The small town centered around the white-steepled church remained the hub of activity, such as it was. Beyond it, tranquillity reigned.

At least that's how Liz saw it right then after being in Woodsley for a grand total of three hours and twenty-seven minutes. Later she'd have reason to reconsider, but let's not get ahead of ourselves.

"Thanks," Debbie said as though she herself was somehow responsible for Woodsley's prettiness. And maybe she *was* in a way, since the combined efforts of the Woodsley clan had helped to make it so. She bagged Liz's groceries with the same special thoroughness she used for Grannie Georgette Eugenia Winston Woodsley, otherwise known as the Holy Terror who would never let you forget it if you so much as squished a single grape by dropping a can of dog food in on top of it.

They chatted a few minutes longer. Debbie felt inspired to tell Liz about all the top spots in town including the movie theater run by her Uncle Thad (showings every Friday night and twice on Saturdays), her aunt May's beauty parlor (pretty good on cuts but watch out if she wants to give you a perm), and, of course, the diner across the street run by her cousin Bart and his wife, Abby (not as good for burgers as the MacDonald's over in Bradford but not bad, either).

Oh, yes, and, by the way, did she know her house, the one she'd bought from Ruth Ann, was supposed to be haunted?

Liz allowed as to how she hadn't known that. "Haunted by whom?" she asked.

"Well," Debbie said. "What happened was that about a hundred, maybe a hundred and fifty years ago, this guy—I don't think he was actually a Woodsley, although he might have been—went kind of nuts one night and chopped up his wife with an axe. They found her body, only without any head, but he disappeared. Supposedly, every once in a while, somebody walking past there thinks they see him with the axe still in his hand standing in front of one of the upstairs windows, probably the same room where he killed her."

She paused for a moment as a thought occurred to her. "Gee, maybe I shouldn't be telling you this."

"It's okay," Liz said. "I'm tough."

Anybody who had gone head-to-head with the boys in the front office wasn't going to let a little thing like an axe-wielding ghost get her down. He stayed out of her way, she'd stay out of his. Otherwise, watch out, buddy, this was a lady with an axe *to grind*.

Debbie gave her a cheerful little wave as she departed. Outside, the light was fading. A slight mist rose from the ponds scattered around town where herons called softly and hawks rustled as they settled down for the night.

Overhead, the first stars twinkled. Liz stopped to look at them. In Washington there were no stars and in other places where she'd been on assignment, she'd never had time to look. After awhile she started feeling a little silly standing there on the sidewalk gawking at the sky so she got back in the car and drove home. It was dark by the time she finished putting the groceries away. She had to let the water run in the bathtub for several minutes before the rust eased off. Once in, she lay back with her eyes closed and did her best not to think. All the same, images darted through her mind—Wheaton looking pompous, Daugherty torn between embarrassment and fear, Wilcox being noble. And behind them all Hauster, who hadn't actually been there; but whose presence was inescapable, grinning at her with his shark smile.

When the water turned tepid, she got out, toweled herself dry, and put on a nightgown. Highly paid television newswomen were probably supposed to wear something more glamorous than cotton nightshirts to sleep in, but that was too bad. She brushed her hair fifty times because her mother had always told her to, then wandered into the bedroom in search of something to do. The quiet was so intense, it made her ears ring. There was a television downstairs, an ancient black and white with a rotary dial that had come with the house, but she wasn't about to turn it on, not and risk hearing something about herself. Fortunately, she'd thought to bring a stack of books. She started one, found it interesting, and read for a while before sleep finally claimed her.

It was maybe an hour after that, around midnight, when the sound woke her. She came out of a deep sleep already stiffening with apprehension. *What in God's name was that?* That soft, flutter-flutter sound coming from over her head?

She sat bolt upright and fumbled for the light beside the bed. Wincing at the sudden glare, she held her breath and forced herself to listen.

Flutter-flutter, whir-whir. It went right on, more intense now and definitely somewhere above her.

Did axe murderers make that kind of noise? Probably not. They'd be more of a *thud-thud* and a maniacal cackle. No, this sounded like birds flying back and forth except hardly any birds did that at night. What flew at night was . . .

That quick darting black thing that had just swooped through her bedroom and out the window she'd thoughtfully left open.

Ai-eeeh!

Her reflexes were still working great. She hit the floor in under a second flat and started squirming her way under the bed only to be stopped by what was probably the largest dustball in the Western hemisphere, a fuzzy mass that looked like it could have been hacked up by a cat the size of Brooklyn.

So much for hiding under the bed. Hey, she hadn't really meant to do that anyway. Not her.

She was Liz Sherwood, intrepid newswoman. She had stood up to bullets, for heaven's sake. She wasn't going to let a little thing like bats scare her, was she?

Watch her. Everybody has their little phobias, the creepy crawlies they'd just rather not deal with. Liz's was bats. It probably had something to do with a trick her brother and his sicko friends had pulled on her back when she was about six and they were all in their Count Dracula phase. Whatever the cause, she was stuck. There was absolutely no way she could handle this on her own.

A-One Auto Repair . . . Abbot Feed and Grain . . . Adler, Deke . . .

She dialed the number, waiting through each excruciatingly slow turn of the rotary dial, and waited again while it rang. Four rings, five, six . . . What if he wasn't home? What did she do then? Sleep outside? How bad could it be? It wasn't *that* cold. Okay, fine, he wasn't there. She could cope, no problem. She'd get a couple of blankets and head for the car. She'd—

"Hello?" Deke said. He sounded groggy, as though he'd been sleeping. Belatedly she remembered that she had been, too, until the attack of the Bat People woke her.

"It's Liz Sherwood. I'm sorry to bother you." Why was she whispering? They couldn't hear her and if the axe-murderer was listening, too bad.

"I know it's late," she said more clearly, "but I've got the same problem as before only more and I don't really know what to do."

If this had been Washington, D.C., there would have been a discussion. *Well, what do you want me to do? Should I come over? Now? Well, all right, maybe I can get a cab. You're sure about this? Bats, uh? Really weird.* And behind all that there would have been a whole other level of meaning. *She turned to him for help, did this mean they were really committed to each other, was he ready for that kind of commitment? Was it really right for him—or for her—at this particular point in their lives? Catching bats was one thing, but what else was she going to expect once he'd done that? Maybe they'd better put the whole thing on ice for a while because after all there was no point rushing into anything, he was only thirty-something, or forty-something and what was the big hurry?*

But this wasn't Washington, D.C., it was Woodsley, and what Deke said was, "I'll be right there."

THREE

"You're lucky," he said awhile later after he'd convinced the three bats he'd found that they really didn't want to live there, after all. "They hadn't actually started nesting. Once they do that, you can be in big trouble. There was a guy over toward Branford who ended up with a couple of hundred in his attic."

"What did he do?" Liz asked. They were in the kitchen. She was wrapped in her big, woolly bathrobe, the same one she'd had since college with her fuzzy slippers on her feet. He was wearing jeans, a plaid workshirt, and workboots. It was a little bit after two A.M. He'd arrived almost immediately after her phone call, but it had taken that long to trap the last of the bats and dump it outside. Liz thought that one had a particularly malevolent glare in his eye (*her* eye?) as he/she zoomed off, but Deke said she was imagining it.

"Bats are actually very benign animals," he told her. "They eat insect pests that can damage crops and they're generally quiet and unobtrusive. If people didn't have this horror-film thing about them, they'd probably be more popular."

"Could be," Liz said dubiously. "So what did the guy do?"

"First he made sure he'd found how they were getting into the house and fixed it so they couldn't. Incidentally, you've got to keep these windows shut until you get screens. Otherwise, they *will* end up nesting."

"They stay locked and bolted," Liz promised. She'd never thought of screens, but he was right. Without them, the house was an open invitation to any animal who happened to wander by and felt like dropping in.

"Then he trapped them in nets and relocated them," Deke said. "You have to be careful around bats because they can carry rabies, but usually they're okay."

"I'll remember that," Liz muttered. She poured two mugs of coffee and carried them over to the table. "Cream, sugar?"

"Black, thanks. Then they cleaned up all the guano. That was really the hard part."

"Guano?"

"What bats leave behind."

"Oh, yeah, guano." What was she *doing* sitting here in the kitchen at two o'clock in the morning talking to the most drop-dead good-looking man she'd ever seen about *bat droppings?* Maybe Wheaton had been right to axe her. Maybe she was totally bananas.

"Bananas?" Liz asked.

"What?"

"Uh, banana cake. I got some at the store. Want a piece?"

He shook his head, looking at her a tad bemusedly. How could a woman look so good in a bathrobe that had come over on the ark and slippers that—they weren't actually alive, were they? They just looked like they could be.

"I really appreciate you doing this," she said.

He shrugged. "We're neighbors. Besides, you're new to all this. You'll get the hang of it quickly enough."

"Maybe, but I'm not sure I'll get the hang of the Woodsleys. Is it my imagination or are we the only two people around here who don't have red hair?"

"Just about. They've been around for quite a while and no matter how many outsiders marry into the clan, it's the Woodsley genes that always seem to end up dominant in the end."

"The woman who sold me this place, Ruth Ann somebody . . ."

"Woodsley Wheaton. She married Jim Wheaton, who was a second or third cousin."

"How do you know that?"

"Because they tell you, that's how. I've lived here five years and I swear I know the pedigree of every single Woodsley around the place. They'll draw a chart for you if you stand still long enough to let them."

"Have you?" What color were his eyes, gray-blue or hazel? She couldn't be sure. They were nice eyes, though, whatever color they were. They looked as though there was always a smile lurking right around the corners.

"Not too often. They're nice people for the most part, but I came up here needing some space for myself."

"How come?"

He hesitated. This wasn't a story he usually told. Still, once you've caught bats for somebody and seen her in her bathrobe, the barriers tended to break down.

"My father wanted me to be a lawyer."

"First, let's kill all the lawyers."

"Shakespeare's *Henry V*, every lawyer's heard the line a hundred times. How about this one? You're driving down the road and you see a dead lawyer and a dead snake. What's the difference?"

"I don't know."

"There are skid marks in front of the snake. Someone really did try to stop."

"Ouch. Okay, here's another. What do you call a hundred dead lawyers at the bottom of the ocean?"

"A good start?"

"You heard it."

"Maybe," Deke said with a grin. She wasn't at all what he'd expected. Anybody who could trade lawyer jokes at two in the morning definitely had something going for her.

"Don't get me wrong," he said, "there are plenty of good lawyers, but I'm not sure Dad was ever one of them. What he was was very successful and very rich. He figured he was doing me a favor to have me end up the same, but I didn't see it that way."

"Why not? There's nothing wrong with having money."

" 'Course not. The problems happen when that's all you've got. I wanted more, not less."

"So you came here and started farming. Did you know anything about it?"

He grinned. "Sure I did. I knew which end of a sheep was which, and I had a pretty fair idea that apples had something to do with the tree of the same name. With that kind of expertise going for me, how could I fail?"

"I give up."

"I worked my butt off night and day and barely made it through the first year. The Woodsleys, all three million of them or however many there are, thought it was a real hoot seeing the city boy scramble, but they also gave me some help, I've got to say that. Anyway, I hung in and after a while things got better."

"No regrets?" Liz asked as she stood up to refill their cups.

He shook his head. "No, I belong here. But what about you? This is a far reach from what you've known."

."I'm not sure about that," she said as she returned to the table. Drinking so much coffee at this hour wasn't smart, but she doubted she'd be able to go back to sleep anyway and he didn't seem to mind. "It's a lot like the town in Texas where I grew up. Everybody knew each other and you had the sense that if something bad happened to you, people would actually care."

"Not like Washington, D.C.?"

"No," she said softly, "not like Washington, D.C. Although to be fair, there are good people there, too. It's like with lawyers. I just happened to hit a major problem that seems to have basically derailed me."

"You mean Hauster?"

Liz nodded. She supposed it was strange to feel so at ease with him, but she couldn't seem to help it. In her experience, handsome men tended to be overly taken with themselves. But Deke wasn't that way at all. He was refreshingly direct and genuinely interested in other people. No wonder he lived way out in the boonies. In the big city he would have been the last living member of an extinct species.

"I goofed," she said.

"You're kidding? The story sounded rock solid to me."

"Oh, the story was. Where I goofed was in not realizing how far Hauster would go to cover it up." She paused, knowing that what she was about to say was incendiary. In the wrong hands it would cause one of those horrible media feeding fits to erupt—the kind she had witnessed often enough but never, ever been part of. Still, she needed to talk. Her entire life had been turned upside down in the past forty-eight hours. If she kept all her feelings about that to herself, she was going to have bats somewhere other than her bedroom.

"All my evidence was stolen," she said quietly, "and my witnesses were intimidated. None of them will say a word on my behalf. I can't prove it, but I think I was set up."

"How so?" Deke asked.

"A man at the network, a very powerful man, asked to see the evidence. I put everything together and stacked it in boxes. With a few minutes to go before our meeting, I went to the ladies' room. While I was gone somebody came into my office and stole the boxes. Maybe I'm being paranoid, but I just think it's too much of a coincidence."

"You're probably right," Deke said. "Besides, there's the whole thing with Hauster and Bank Northeastern."

Liz's eyes widened slightly. "What thing?"

"Hauster's in so deep with Northeastern that they can't possibly stand by and let him fold. Since they were the principal financial backer on the leveraged buy-out of your network last year, it stands to reason they'd have enough clout to do damage control on your story. If you were set up, and my guess is you were, there was strong motivation for it."

"I'm sorry," Liz said. "I must have missed something. How could you know this? I spent a month researching the Hauster story and I didn't turn up anything about Northeastern."

"They've kept their ties to him very quiet," Deke said matter-of-factly, "but they run deep all the same."

"How do you know?" Liz persisted. Maybe she was dreaming, but it looked as though he flushed slightly.

"I didn't become a lawyer," he said, "but I did start a little investment fund using a nest egg left me by my grandmother. One thing led to another and we ended up not doing too badly."

"What was the name of the fund?"

He told her. If there had still been bats in the

house, they could have flown into Liz's mouth, at least until she remembered to close it. Score one for her, crackerjack newswoman. She thought he was a hayseed sheep farmer who happened to be good at catching bats and devastatingly attractive in the bargain. But not too long ago he'd been one of the wonder kids of Wall Street. He'd made billions—with a b—for people smart enough to trust him with their money. And then he'd simply disappeared. One day he was there and the next he wasn't. His clients were paid off big and they clamored for him to return, but he never did. It was over and done with, end of the story.

"Oh," she said.

"You got to try things before you realize they aren't really for you," he said.

"Is that what you're doing now, trying something?"

"No, this one's for real. I found what I was looking for." At least, pretty much. He still had that little fantasy going about the wife and kids, the whole ball of wax, but he wasn't crazy enough to say anything about that to her. She was looking spooked enough as it was.

"If I had known about Hauster and the tie to the network," she said, "I might have handled things differently."

"You mean killed the story?"

He didn't pull any punches, that was for sure. If she had known, she could have kept her mouth shut, held on to her job, and still been in line for anchor. Instead, she was sitting in here in the boonies, dodging bats and trying not to read too much significance into the fact that for the first time in a very long time she was seriously attracted to a man who, as he himself had said, knew which end of a sheep was which.

"No," she said, "I wouldn't have killed it." Knowing that made her feel good. She would have gone the distance no matter what. The folks back in Abilene would be proud of her. Only problem was that she still had to get through the rest of her life.

Deke looked at her for a long moment. He nodded. "No, you wouldn't have."

Silence fell. There they sat, staring at each other, while outside the spindly-limbed trees rustled, murmuring of the promise of leafier times soon to come.

"I'd better be going," Deke said. "It's late."

They both got up at the same time, scraping their chairs back. Liz walked him to the door.

"I can't tell you how much I appreciate what you did," she said. "If you hadn't come over, I'd be sleeping in the car."

"I did that one summer when I was driving cross-country. My back hasn't straightened out yet."

"How old were you?"

"Sixteen." At her surprise, he smiled. "But that's another story. Have dinner with me tomorrow?"

The invitation was unexpected, although with hindsight she should have seen it coming. They were both single and clearly attracted to each other. At least she was to him; it was harder to tell how he felt. He kept more inside, while whatever went through her mind tended to come out her mouth. Over the years she'd learned to put a brake on that, but sometimes it slipped.

"Why?" she asked.

It was his turn to look surprised. "Because I figure we'd both enjoy it, and you have to eat anyway."

Simple. No fuss, no muss, and especially no pressure.

"Okay," Liz said because it just wasn't in her to turn down such a gracious invitation.

Deke nodded again and took himself off. After awhile, the sound of the truck coughing and wheezing died away down the road. Nothing was left except the bats talking to each other in the trees in that high-pitched whistle Liz couldn't hear but could feel along her skin. What they were saying she didn't dare imagine.

She went back into the house, made sure all the windows were securely locked, and fell back into bed. With two cups of stand-up coffee perking through her, a real man to contemplate complete with an invitation to dinner, and her life in turmoil she didn't really expect to sleep. She'd just close her eyes for a minute.

Several hours later, the phone woke her. It was light outside, not the faint gray light of early dawn but the full-blown glare of day. The clock said 7:08 A.M. Birds were singing in the trees; she could hear them even through the closed windows. Dust motes danced in the rays of sun streaming through the thin cotton curtains. The sky was blue, the air radiant.

And the phone was still ringing.

"Huh? What?" Liz wasn't at her best first thing in the morning. The woman on the other end of the line already knew that. She didn't care.

"You!" she screamed. "You're there! I can't believe it. I've been trying everywhere. I finally remembered you bought the godforsaken place in North Carolina. You can't believe what I went through finding the number. What are you thinking of? What have you *done?*"

Liz held the receiver a few inches away from her ear, looked to the ceiling as a source of divine patience, and said, "Virginia. I'm in Virginia, not North Carolina, and I'm fine, thanks for asking. How are you, Vivian?"

"How am I? How do you think I am? My star client, my best friend, practically my sister, pulls the stupidest stunt of all time and you ask me how I am? Devastated, that's how. I was on the phone for an hour with Wheaton, that slime. You know they're reneging on your entire contract?"

"I know," Liz said calmly. There was a provision in her contract that she could be dismissed before it expired, but in that case, the remaining portions of her considerable salary had to be paid *unless* she had "committed grievous wrong against the integrity of the network". In their book, she had.

"Whatta you mean, you know? Are you crazy? This is major league. With them taking that position, nobody in the business will touch you. Already, the word's out that you're poison."

"Fine, good, I couldn't care less." Not true that, but she was in no mood to own up to how much it hurt to be suckered the way she'd been. "Hauster got me, there's nothing I can do about that. After eight years with the network and a couple of hundred major stories, they refuse to believe me. So I'm out. Those are the breaks."

"You're talking about an entire career! Not to mention the money! You've got to fight."

"With what? The evidence is gone, the witnesses have high-tailed it, there's nothing left. Besides, Hauster and the network are in each other's pockets."

"What?" Vivian gasped. Even in her cynical, hard-bitten world, this was a bit much. "What are you saying?"

"You heard me and no, I won't tell you how I know, I just do. There's no way out of this, Viv, and I'm tired of fighting anyway. I needed a rest even before this happened. Now it looks as though I'm going to get a nice long one.''

"Think about what you're saying. Your career's been your life. What're you going to do without it?''

Good question. Too bad Liz didn't have a good answer. "I don't know," she admitted. "But Virginia's more interesting than I thought it would be. I've got enough money to live on for some time. Maybe I'll just try enjoying myself.''

"It'll never work," the loving agent said. "You'll drive yourself batty.''

"Please, no bat jokes. Look, what am I supposed to do? With the situation the way it is, are you telling me you can get me work somewhere?''

"Well, no, not exactly. But you could try the lecture circuit, tell your side of the story to the public. You have a lot of fans and Hauster has none. Maybe a letter-writing campaign could—''

"No," Liz said quickly, sensing a plan in the making and one she wanted no part of. "Hauster doesn't need fans, he's got power, plain and simple. Besides, I like it here. This is going to be good for me.''

"Batty," Vivian said again. "Stark raving. You won't last a week.''

"We'll see. Thanks for calling.''

"Stay in touch!" Vivian hollered down the line as Liz hung up. She lay back for a moment, stretching under the covers, and smiled. After the anguish and rage of recent days, an unexpected sense of freedom was settling over her. For the first time since she was a kid, she didn't have a job to go to. Nobody was counting on her, expecting her to come through, looking to her to lead the pack. She could stay in bed all day if she wanted to but she didn't. She had things to do.

This time the list was longer: get screens in, buy paint, clean!

The screens were in the basement. The same guy who sold her the paint down at Woodsley Hardware agreed to install the screens. While he was doing that, she scrubbed the walls in the downstairs rooms. Earlier, she'd swept and dusted. By the end of the day when she finished painting the kitchen, she was sore all over but filled with an unmistakable sense of satisfaction. She slept well—with fresh air and without bats—and got up early the next morning. By midafternoon she had the front hall and the living room finished and was ready to start upstairs. The place was actually starting to look livable, but her body was beginning to protest. It was time to quit.

She soaked in the tub, a claw-footed porcelain Victorian, and stood in front of the closet for a time trying to decide what to wear. The two suitcases she'd brought seemed like they ought to be more than ample, but she wasn't sure what dinner with a former financial whiz turned sheep farmer called for. She settled finally on a plaid skirt and sweater that were simple but pretty and suitable to the cool evening. At the last minute she left her hair down and added a squirt of Chanel. In the mirror, she saw that she looked softer than usual and more relaxed than she had in months, if not longer.

"Looking good, kid," she murmured. Her confidence needed the boost, such as it was.

She needed it even more a while later when she opened the door for Deke and found him standing there in a blue blazer and gray slacks, looking as though he'd just stepped out of the pages of some magazine instead of off the farm. Heaven help her, the man made little tingly bursts of excitement ricochet along her spine. She was fifteen again and sweet on Tommy Martin, the hunk down the block who hadn't known she was alive. Except at fifteen she wasn't capable of the feeling she had in her now, and Tommy Martin had been less than a pale shadow to the likes of Deke Adler.

"That's a nice outfit," he said as she shut the door behind them.

She murmured her thanks and accepted his help getting into the truck. His hand on the small of her back made the tinglies worse.

Get a grip, girl, she told herself, but it didn't work. What she'd known of reality wasn't holding up too well out here in bat land. She curled her fingers around the edges of the seat and held on as the truck lurched off into the night.

FOUR

"Do you like horses?" Deke asked.

"What, to eat?"

He shot her a startled look. "Of course not. We don't eat horses in Virginia. What made you think of that?"

"We're on our way to dinner so I was thinking about eating and then you said horses, so I—" She broke off and stared straight ahead at the windshield as though the nothing she could see was the most interesting nothing she'd ever not seen. "I guess I'm a little nervous."

"Why?" Deke asked.

"You should have been a reporter, you know? Always with the questions."

"You don't have to answer if you don't want to," he pointed out reasonably.

True enough, but it wasn't exactly the way to begin an evening. "All right," she said. "I'm a little nervous because it's been a long time since I went out on a date."

He eased up on the gas a little and stared at her. "You're kidding?"

"Why would I kid about a thing like that? It's the truth, I haven't been dating."

"Neither have I."

It was her turn to be startled. "What?"

"This is the first date I've been on in more than a year."

"How come?"

"I don't know exactly, it just seemed to work out that way. I think I got tired of going through the motions. And then I have been busy with the farm. A tendency to fall asleep before ten in the evening cuts down on your social life."

Liz laughed. She was relieved as well as surprised. Men she knew, even the smarter ones, would rip out their tongues rather than admit they weren't living some macho fantasy. Deke was a whole lot more straightforward than that.

"So how come you decided to step out tonight?" she asked.

His hands tightened slightly on the steering wheel. A long time back, when he was still wet behind the ears, he'd decided on honesty not only as the best policy but also as the best defense. It cut down on the misunderstandings, the conflicts, and all the other nonsense he'd seen his parents live with. But that didn't make it easy.

"I'm very attracted to you," he said quietly. "It's been a long time since I felt anything like that. You're beautiful, but there's something else about you, something inside, that I'd like to get to know better."

"Oh," Liz said.

Before she could say anything else, Deke turned the tables. "Why did you accept?"

"Pretty much the same reason."

"Yeah?" He looked pleased. His eyes—it turned out they were gray-blue—crinkled up at the corners.

She smiled and settled back more comfortably. "Yeah."

He was silent for a moment, thinking that over, before he slipped a tape into the cassette player. The lilting strands of Vivaldi's "Spring" floated out into the Virginia night. It was one of Liz's favorite pieces that she listened to whenever she was working on a particularly tough assignment. Finding it here in this place and time only added to the growing sense of rightness.

"Yes," she said. "I do like horses—to ride."

"Good. I've got a couple. You're welcome to borrow one anytime you like. They can always use the exercise."

"I just might do that once I get the house fixed up."

"How's that going?"

"Pretty good. I got the screens in and I've painted the downstairs."

"Hey, that *is* good. How do you like the place?"

"A whole lot more than I did two days ago."

He laughed at that and they drove on through the darkness with the Vivaldi rippling around them and the rare, sweet sense of rightness clinging to them. But there was something else, too, the need for each other that was just beginning, but was already stronger than either had ever known. Frightening it was, but exhilarating as well. Stars gleamed overhead, and off to the east a full moon was rising. Light from it spilled over the countryside, along the winding ribbon of road, leading them onward.

They went to Denny's which was a small, country-style restaurant outside of Bradford. The menu was simple—chicken and ribs, decent steaks, and surprisingly good grilled fish. They had the sole and the house wine, and they danced. The music was slow, soothing, and sensual. Deke was a good dancer—easy, not pushy. Liz had never thought of herself as much skilled in that area, but with him she felt as though she fit. The rightness again.

When they finished dinner, they stayed on for a while to dance some more. She liked the warmth of him and the way he smelled of soap and leather and something intrinsically himself. Men she had known in Washington, D.C., smelled of expensive cologne if they smelled of anything at all. She had to stop comparing everything here to the big city, but the temptation was strong. It was all so different. *She* was so different.

It was ten-thirty before they left the restaurant. She teased him about being up so late. He laughed and said maybe he'd regret it in the morning, but it was worth it. He drove her home through darkness so hushed she could hardly bear to break it.

At the door, she hesitated a moment before suggesting he come in for coffee. He hesitated, too, before shaking his head. "I'd like to," he said, "but I really do have to get up early."

Liz was a little taken aback by that. It was usually the woman's decision whether to offer an invitation. The man almost always accepted, which got them both into the whole thing about what the invitation really meant, just coffee, or did he expect more, or did she? It was all rather tiresome and she found herself unexpectedly relieved at being spared it. Yet also disappointed. She liked being with him. He was good company . . . and then there were those tingly bursts he kept setting off in her.

"You're sure?" she asked.

He nodded. "I had a good time."

"So did I."

"Let's do it again."

"Let's."

He lowered his head. A steely arm drifted around her waist. "Soon."

"Soon," she agreed, and felt the quick brush of his mouth, hard but not demanding. Instinctively, she relaxed against him, giving herself up to the pleasure he evoked. A soft sigh escaped her.

The kiss deepened. Deke had meant to keep it light. He'd been around the block too many times to believe in rushing anything. They were getting along fine, he really liked her, and he could tell it was mutual. But the feeling was fragile and he wanted to give it time to take root.

Which was all well and good in theory but didn't allow for the driving urge he felt to know this woman in the most fundamental way possible. Over dinner, watching her in the candlelight, he thought she looked amazingly young and untouched for what she'd been through. She retained an intrinsic innocence he found enthralling.

A tremor raced through him, answered by her own. They strained closer, her breasts brushing the hard contours of his chest. He tasted her, savoring her sweetness, wanting more. Much, much more.

Shakily, he raised his head. Smoke swirled in his eyes, hinting at the fire raging deep.

"I didn't expect that," he said.

"Neither did I." Her voice quivered slightly.

Slowly he released her and took a step back. Their eyes met. Liz's were a bit glazed. She took a quick breath and another, and held out her hand just the way her mother had taught her way back in Abilene, in the days when there were still nice little white gloves to be worn and nice little girls who actually wore them.

"Thank you for a very nice evening."

They shook, once up and down, very solemnly while they eyed each other. His mouth quirked.

"Thank *you*," he said, very properly. He'd had some rearing, too, even if it had been catch-as-catch-can.

They stood, neither moving, until it occurred to Liz that he wasn't leaving until she was safe and sound inside. The old-fashioned courtliness of that touched her. She was smiling when she shut the door behind her after one last good night.

The smile lingered as she prepared for bed and it followed her into sleep.

It was still with her the next morning when she awoke. She actually caught herself humming as she pulled on jeans and an old shirt. The incongruity of such simple pleasure after so many years of seriousness made her laugh out loud. If anyone could see her, they'd think Viv had been right, she was bats. But she felt deep-down happy and filled with anticipation in a way she hadn't been for a very long time.

She spent the morning painting the bedroom. When that was done she fixed a simple lunch and decided to have it outside. The garden was an overgrown tangle, but it had possibilities. She was munching an apple and thinking about putting in vegetables when she heard a car coming up the driveway. A door slammed, feet crunched, and a cheery voice called, "Halloo, anyone here?"

Liz came around the side of the house to confront a large, red-headed woman bearing down on her. The woman held a pie thrust out between her hands. She had small coal-black eyes and a mile-wide smile.

"I'm Agnes Woodsley," she said, "Woodsley's unofficial welcoming committee, and you're Liz Sherwood. We know all about you. Such a pleasure to have you here. I hope you like rhubarb."

"Love it," Liz said automatically. She took the pie before it could be stuck into her solar plexus. Because it was clearly expected, she said, "Please come in."

Agnes was delighted to do so. Once inside, her head swiveled back and forth, taking in everything Liz had done. "Nice," she said. "very nice. I would have been by sooner, but I heard you were working your butt off. Jake said you bought enough paint to do the Brooklyn Bridge. Whatever you don't open, be sure to take back to him. He'll give you a credit."

"I'll remember that," Liz said bemusedly. Agnes Woodsley was short, built like a linebacker; and positively exuded cheerfulness. She followed Liz into the kitchen, nodded some more, and accepted the offer of coffee "if it's already made".

It wasn't, but Liz felt compelled to assure that her making a pot wouldn't be any trouble, that she'd just been thinking about doing it anyway and please do sit down. That was the trouble with good manners. Once they were drummed into you in childhood, you were pretty well stuck with them all the way through.

Agnes lowered her ample bulk onto one of the ladder-back chairs and shifted around until she got comfortable. "Jake also said you were worried about bats. No call. They give you any trouble, just get yourself a tennis racquet and have at 'em. A couple of good whacks is all it takes."

"I don't think I'd actually want to kill them," Liz said. "I just don't want them moving in with me."

"Don't know what else you're gonna do. There's times you gotta be tough."

"A friend of mine was nice enough to catch them and put them outside. I haven't had any problem since."

Agnes's antennae went up. Liz could almost see them twitching. "Friend? Didn't know you knew anybody in these parts 'cept for Ruth Ann."

"I met Deke Adler from down the road," Liz

admitted, already wishing she hadn't mentioned it. Agnes seized on that like a dog with a bone that was just begging to be chewed.

"Deke? Land o' goshen, girl, why didn't you say so?"

Liz thought she just had, but she forebore mentioning it. Instead, she brought the coffee over to the table and sat down.

"It certainly is beautiful here," she said, hoping to steer her guest onto a more neutral subject.

Agnes took a quick swallow of the coffee, unfazed by the fact that it was steaming hot, and ignored the hint. Her eyes gleamed. "He's just about the dishiest thing ever to come through here. Been trying to fix him up with one of my nieces, I got thirty-seven of 'em at last count. But he doesn't seem interested."

Liz murmured something noncommittal which Agnes took as encouragement to keep going. Or maybe she didn't need any urging. With the bit between her teeth, she was off and running.

"He's never been married, he told Ruth Ann that when she sold him his place. Drove a hard bargain, too. Knows the value of a dollar." Implicit in that, at least to Liz's ears, was the suggestion that the same couldn't be said for every city slicker who came wandering by, checkbook in hand, particularly not highly paid television newswomen with a yen for a country getaway.

"You ever been hitched?" she asked.

Liz shook her head. "No, you?" Turnabout was fair game. If Agnes wanted to ask questions, she could answer a few, too.

"Three times. Buried two of 'em and had one run off. Darned if he wasn't my favorite, too. Oh, well, you can't have everything in this life. You still think Hauster's going broke?"

Three husbands, thirty-seven nieces, and a tolerance for two-thousand-degree coffee. Clearly Agnes Woodsley was a woman to watch out for.

"Beats me. The girl at the checkout, Debbie, told me somebody got killed in this house. Is that true?"

Agnes chuckled. The idea seemed to amuse her. "She tell you that old chestnut about the axe murder?"

"Uh . . . something like that. It's not true then?"

"Sure it is, only it wasn't the wife that got killed, it was her lover. Old Hiram Whirter Woodsley came home a couple of days early from a trip to Boston and caught them together. The wife hightailed it. She was a Bernard from over toward Bradford, by the way. Went back to her family, she did. But the man . . . well, they never did find most of him."

"He killed him here?" Liz asked. Somehow, when Debbie told it, it didn't seem so bad, but now the idea of somebody getting axed in her very own house was less than appealing.

" 'Course not," Agnes said. "This house hadn't even been built back then. Chester Woodsley, my great-great-grandfather on my mother's side, built it back in '02. The murder was old news by then."

"I should think so," Liz said with relief.

" 'Course Hiram was Chester's brother and he was still alive back then, so he probably visited here from time to time. Could have sat right here in this very room for all I know."

"You mean he never went to jail for the killing?" Liz asked.

Agnes shrugged. "Guess not. They never did find a body, just a pair of pants. There were people who claimed they saw a fellow running buck naked down the road, but who knows? Maybe Hiram killed him, maybe he didn't. Least ways, he never did say."

"You'd have thought he'd want to get that straightened out," Liz murmured.

"Oh, I don't know. My third cousin, Daniel Wiggins II, went around for years talking to people who weren't there and he never felt he had to explain about that. Had nice long conversations, he did. Got some good tips on the races, too. So, you setting your cap for Deke or what?"

"I . . . uh . . . no, of course not. I barely know the man. Besides, do people actually set their cap anymore? I thought it all kind of happened by accident if it happened at all."

Agnes rolled her eyes heavenward. "That's the trouble nowadays. Young people have no idea how things really work. They always end up surprised when life turns around all of a sudden and bites 'em on the butt."

"I've been bitten plenty," Liz said dryly. "I could be sitting on steel by now. Don't worry, Deke's still fair game for your nieces and anyone else you want to throw his way."

"Not me," Agnes said. "I make it my business never to intrude." She said it with a straight face, too, which was pretty good all things considered. "You coming to the church social?"

"Not that I know of."

"It's Saturday night at the hall next to the church. Everybody'll be there. Be a nice chance for you to meet people."

"I'd like to, but—"

"Get Deke to bring you. He always drops by." She stood up, groaning slightly, and headed for the door.

When she was gone Liz went back to the garden, stared at it awhile longer, and tried to decide whether or not she was up to painting the upstairs bathroom. She was starting to pull the drop cloths in that direction when the phone rang.

It was Deke. "Hi," he said. "Want to see a lamb born?"

FIVE

"It's little late in the year for this," Deke said as he bent over the ewe, coaxing her gently. "But that's how it happens sometimes."

Liz knelt beside him in the bed of fresh straw. Her eyes were saucer wide and her hands shook. She'd never seen anything born before. It was an incredible sight.

Lambs did it a little differently than people. A leg came first, followed by another. The ewe strained and Deke gave her some help, gently easing the little fellow out. It came out all dark and slick, and bigger than Liz would have thought possible. In a moment or two, the ewe was licking it efficiently while the lamb snuggled close.

"How wonderful," Liz murmured. In the gray light of the sheep barn, the rest of the world

seemed far away. She was conscious of sunlight
glancing off the straw, turning it golden, of silence
so thick it made her whisper, and most of all of
Deke, strong and warm beside her, soothing the
ewe with the touch of his hand.

"Really something, isn't it?" he asked.

She nodded. "It's beautiful."

He was relieved. When he called her, it was on
the spur of the moment. He was a little surprised
she said she'd come and then even more so by
how calm and capable she was through the whole
thing. Now he was glad she'd seen the beauty of
it, glad that he'd thought to call her, and glad
especially that they were sharing so simple but
special a moment.

"I never really get used to it," he said, "no
matter how many times I see an animal born. It
always seems like a miracle."

"Maybe it always is."

They sat for a while in the straw, watching as
the lamb suckled. When it had settled down to
sleep, they went back to the house together.

Deke lived in a rambling farm house he described as "built between 1850 and yesterday".
At one time it had housed upward of twelve people. There were bedrooms galore, three full baths,
a kitchen complete with fireplace, and a living
room that looked out over a wide deck and beyond
to rolling fields.

Deke excused himself to get cleaned up. When

he came back a few minutes later, Liz was standing at the living-room window enjoying the view.

"This is fantastic," she said, and meant it.

"It's too big, but it came with great acreage. I couldn't resist."

"That's not what Agnes says. She says you drove a hard bargain."

He laughed. "Has she been by to visit you?"

"Her and her rhubarb pie."

"Watch out. She'll be looking to fix you up with someone."

"Hmm, she did mention something along that line. Seems like you and her thirty-seven nieces haven't hit it off."

A look of mock horror crossed his face. "Is that how many there are? I'm doomed."

"Not necessarily." He looked so good standing there with his chestnut hair still damp, the sleeves of an old plaid shirt rolled up to reveal muscled forearms burnished by the sun. He exuded masculinity and more—confidence, honesty, strength.

She glanced away for a moment, took a deep breath and said, "I was thinking of going to the church social Saturday. Want to come with me?"

Thirty years old and she'd never asked a man for a date before. How *did* they do it? But, of course, they were expected to so maybe that made it easier. For her it was tough. Her heart was beating fast and a knot started growing at the pit of her stomach.

It didn't help that Deke looked surprised, but unlike her, it wasn't his first time. Women had asked him out before, not often but enough for him to know that after the initial shock it was kind of nice.

Besides, he'd been thinking of asking her to go with him anyway.

"Sure," he said.

"Oh . . ." She hadn't expected it to be that simple. "Good, fine, uh . . . should I pick you up?"

He laughed again. "You can if you want, but you've got to admit the truck has a certain something you just don't get in that fancy sports car of yours."

Which she took to mean he'd rather she didn't. Truth be told, she wasn't quite ready for that much role reversal herself. "The truck's fine."

"Good. Want some coffee?"

She shook her head. "I really should get back. I was just starting to paint the bathroom when Agnes dropped in. And then you called. If I hurry, I can still finish it today."

"You can," he agreed, "but do you necessarily have to? You could take it a little easier."

That was a novel thought. She was so used to doing everything as quickly as possible that the idea of slowing down took some getting used to. "I suppose I could," she said, but doubtfully.

"The bathroom won't go anywhere. I can vouch

for that. If you want to do something, how about coming for a ride with me?''

There was definitely more appeal to that than getting plopped in the eye with Summer Beige latex.

"Okay."

Back behind the sheep barn was a stable. The scent of hay and well-cared for tack lingered in the late-afternoon air. Beyond, in a paddock, a pair of horses grazed leisurely. They lifted their heads when they saw Deke and came trotting toward him. He patted their muzzles gently as they poked at his pockets, seeking a treat.

"Sorry, fellows," he said, "no apples. How about a little exercise instead?"

They seemed agreeable enough, standing quietly as they were saddled. Liz hadn't ridden in years, but it came back to her quickly. They moved off at a slow trot. The sun was turning westward, suffusing the air with a golden hue. A cooling breeze carried scents of the stirring earth. For a time they rode in contented silence. When they drew rein finally near a small lake, Deke laid a hand on her arm and pointed without speaking. At the edge of the water, half hidden but still discernible, a small red fox crouched to drink.

"They're coming back," Deke murmured. "So are the eagles and some of the other birds that were almost lost. We've even got a couple of beavers on the stream near the house."

Liz smiled but she didn't speak. She was too caught up in the beauty of the moment. The fox scampered off as they dismounted. Hand in hand, she and Deke walked along the edge of the pond. They left the horses to graze and climbed a small outcropping of rock. At the top of it, a pine tree grew. Its roots had carved a deep crevice in which moss and lichens flourished. They sat with their backs to the tree and looked out over the pond. A heron swooped low, seeking dinner in the silver flash of fish darting close to the surface.

Deke's hand was warm on hers. His touch was undemanding and somehow reassuring. She took a deep breath, let it out, and felt her eyes closing.

"Sleepy?" he asked indulgently.

"A little," she admitted. "All that work around the house must have worn me out more than I thought." The fresh air, the fading sun, and the effects of healthy exercise were all combining to make her feel groggy.

He moved slightly, drawing her into the curve of his arm. Her head rested on his broad chest. She could feel the beat of his heart beneath her cheek. An insect droned near her ear only to be brushed away. She thought she felt the gentle touch of lips on her forehead but she couldn't be sure. .She didn't expect to sleep. It was a small quirk of her nature that she couldn't do so unless she was alone. As a consequence, she had never actually "slept" with anyone since becoming an adult and leaving home. She wouldn't sleep, she would just relax. It was so pleasant lying this way in his arms, so safe and secure. She couldn't remember the last time she had felt so cared for. She really ought to tell him so. In a little while she'd open her eyes but not just yet. It was so pleasant . . . so very . . .

She slept. Deke smiled to himself. He didn't really know, but he did sense that such behavior was unusual for her. She was so filled with vitality. Despite what had happened to her, she had a core of strength and determination he couldn't help but admire. Weak, clinging women—or those who pretended to be—sent him running for the nearest door. But Liz had exactly the opposite effect. Sitting there with her in his arms, looking out over the tranquil pond, he felt a degree of happiness so profound that it almost alarmed him. He had not thought of himself as lonely but now he realized the gap in his life had been even bigger than he'd thought. She changed that, this plain-speaking woman whose natural honesty was her greatest strength and greatest vulnerability.

He thought of Hauster and shook his head in disgust. On the one hand, he would have liked the man to appear before him so he could express more adequately—and physically—what he thought about his treatment of Liz. On the other hand, he had Hauster to thank, however inadvertently, for bringing her to him.

Or, more correctly, bringing her to Woodsley, for she was not truly with him yet. In his arms, yes, and he had tasted the sweetness of her mouth. But he wanted more. Far more.

He settled himself more comfortably against the tree and began to consider exactly what that meant.

The cooling air woke Liz. She stirred reluctantly. There was something hard and warm under her cheek. Memory flooded back. She sat up quickly. "I'm sorry . . . I didn't realize . . ."

"That's all right. You looked like you needed it. But we'd better be heading back. It's starting to cool off."

In fact, it was getting cold, Liz was glad she had on a sweater as they remounted and started back toward the house. By the time they got there, night was coming on fast.

"Go on inside," Deke said when he caught her shivering. He insisted on taking care of the horses by himself, joining her a short time later. He found her in the kitchen standing in front of the cold fireplace.

"That's not doing you any good," he said.

"It's getting late. I should be getting back."

"You could stay," he suggested. As he spoke, he struck a match and tossed it onto the fire. It caught immediately. Within moments a cheerful blaze was warming the room.

"For dinner?" she asked, a bit warily. She'd come to Woodsley to get away from all the upset and turmoil her life had suddenly become. But instead of refuge she seemed to have run smack into a speeding locomotive of her own emotions. She just wasn't ready for that—or at least she didn't think she was.

He met her eyes candidly, as though he understood everything she was thinking. "Dinner."

The corners of her mouth lifted. "I hope that means you can cook because I'm a total washout in the kitchen. Actually, that isn't quite true. I can boil water but only in the microwave."

"Too bad I don't have one. How about you just watch?"

Liz settled on a stool in front of the counter. He moved around the kitchen with the same easy grace she had noticed he brought to everything else. A knife flashed effortlessly as he sliced chicken, mushrooms, and scallions.

"Stir fry okay?" he asked.

"Sure. How long have you been cooking?"

"Since I was about six. My grandmother taught me."

"That's unusual, isn't it?"

"Probably," he agreed. "But she was a pretty feisty lady. A little thing like social convention never got in her way.

"Did you ever get teased about it, a boy knowing how to cook?"

"Sure, but I found out pretty fast that you can make more friends with shrimp in beurre blanc sauce than you can without it."

"What's that?" Liz asked.

"Shrimp in butter and white wine with a dash of cayenne pepper."

"Sounds delicious."

"It is. I'll fix it for you sometime. Hand me that box of rice, will you?"

She did, and a half hour or so later, dinner was ready. They ate at the big pine table in front of the kitchen fireplace. Deke poured a crisp Chablis to go with the chicken and vegetables, the fire crackled, Vivaldi played in the background, and Liz began to seriously consider the possibility that she was in over her head and sinking fast.

So *this* was where the real men had gone. They were hiding in the woods raising sheep and cooking stir fry. Did that mean she had a duty to return to Washington, D.C., and tell all the women there what she'd discovered? Would that, in turn, prompt an exodus from the big city to such places as Deer Flat, Montana, and Outer Bank, Alaska, where other real men had been rumored sighted?

"What are you thinking about?" Deke asked.

"Men and women."

"Oh, good. You had kind of a faraway look in your eye."

"It's different in the city."

"No kidding. Listen, if you come up with any

TUNE IN TOMORROW / 97

more bits of revealed wisdom like that, you be sure to share them."

She shook her head ruefully, knowing she must sound silly and not caring. Holy cow, that was a change. She'd spent years trying to be taken seriously and now suddenly that didn't matter anymore.

"How much of this wine have I had?" she asked, looking at her glass suspiciously.

"About two sips. Why?"

"I don't know exactly. I'm just feeling . . . different."

He looked at her for a long moment before his eyes crinkled about around the edges. "There are strawberries for dessert. If you're a good girl, I'll let you help me dip them in melted chocolate."

Liz groaned. She was going down for the third time and she didn't even care. There must be something in the air.

"All right," she said.

She cleared away the dishes while Deke set a double boiler on the stove. He shaved long curls of dark chocolate into it, stirring until they dissolved. From the refrigerator, he took strawberries the size of small plums with their green tops still attached.

"A friend of mine grows these in Florida. He sends me a couple of cases every year."

"Nice friend," Liz murmured.

"Have you done this before?"

"Does it look like water in a microwave?"

"Guess not. Okay, it's easy." He took a hand, eased a strawberry between her fingers, and lowered it toward the chocolate. "Just give it a swirl."

"Like that?"

"Perfect. Now set it on the wax paper."

"You really do this for fun? I mean when you're alone?"

"Of course not. It isn't worth doing without someone to help. Also, eating chocolate alone is a sin."

"Oh, yeah, I forgot that."

She did another, still with his help. She liked the way his touch felt better and better every time she experienced it. He was standing very close to her. If she leaned back just the littlest bit, she could feel the lean strength of his body all along the length of her own.

"Oops," she said, "I got too much on that one."

"That's okay. Just think, now you'll be able to say you know how to boil water—in a micro-wave—plus dip strawberries."

"A woman of many accomplishments, that's me."

"Hmm, what's that perfume I smell?"

" 'Lalique, but it's a shampoo, not a perfume."

"You have beautiful hair."

"Oh . . . thank you."

Her hand shook slightly as she laid the last strawberry on the wax paper. He reached around her to switch off the burner under the chocolate. "They need to sit for a while," he said.

"Do they?" Her voice sounded breathless. His fingers moved slightly over the curve of her cheek, along the sensitive line of the throat. She shivered.

"Cold?" he asked.

"No, not cold." Not at all. Heat simmered through her. She swayed slightly as though drawn to him by a force she could not resist.

She felt the brush of his mouth against her skin. A soft moan broke from her as her head tipped back. His arms enclosed her, his hands spread across her rib cage, moving upward to envelop her breasts.

"So beautiful," he murmured.

She shut her eyes, breathing in the mingled scents of chocolate and strawberries, warm male skin and the fire crackling, wood smoke dancing, night falling, life entwining round her, drawing her into the light.

She shouldn't, she hardly knew him, it was madness. Sweet, needful madness. She turned in his arms, her palms pressed against his chest. Strength radiated through the tips of her fingers. His touch hardened. He lowered his head and claimed her mouth.

The kiss was beyond anything they had shared before. The sudden explosiveness of it caught them both by surprise. His tongue plunged deeply, demanding acquiescence, taking, tormenting, making her long for more.

Her hands tightened on his shoulders, the nails raking him. He groaned and bent slightly, sweeping her up. There was time still to think, to consider, but neither of them took it. She lay, unresisting, her head against his chest as he crossed the room.

Stairs fell away below them. She had a distant impression of the second floor and a room that was large, warm, and welcoming. The bed was an antique pencil-post so high it had to be reached by a stepping stool. At least Liz would have had to use the stool had she not been gently deposited in the center of the bed.

She felt the mattress depress under him. He knelt above her, watching through smokey eyes as a pulse beat in her throat. "Liz, are you sure . . . ?"

He was so careful, even now giving her the chance to say no. He made her feel so safe, as she had not in so very long. Reason faded, rushing beyond her reach. Nothing remained except him and the driving need he made her feel.

Her answer was the whisper of his name on her lips and the swift touch of her fingers along the buttons of his shirt. She undid them one by one, revealing burnished skin and sculpted muscles. He was so beautiful that her breath caught in her throat. Her hands moved over him, exploring, learning, until his control broke.

He lifted her easily, drawing her to him, and quickly stripped away her sweater she had put on so long ago in the morning of another lifetime. Beneath it she wore only a soft cotton camisole. She had done without a bra for comfort, but now there was none, only hunger raging, making her grasp his hands and pull them to her.

He groaned deep in his throat. Her breasts nestled in his big, calloused palms, the thumbs rubbing over her aching nipples. Sweet, hot pleasure tore through her. She arched against him, rubbing against the smooth hardness of his chest.

He lowered her again onto her back. Above her, eyes holding hers, he removed her shoes and socks. His fingers rubbed the arches of her feet, digging in slightly and sending little rays of pleasure bursting along her spine. He laughed at her moan of unfettered delight, but his smile gave way to tension as he removed her jeans. She was left in the camisole and bikini pants that hid little from his gaze.

His shirt fell on the floor beside the bed with her clothes. He turned away for a moment to remove his shoes, then stood and, facing her, unsnapped his pants. Her tongue moistened her lips. She reached out and slowly drew the zipper down. Beneath her hand she felt his burgeoning hardness.

She rose on the bed, kneeling and watched as

he slipped out of the pants. Naked, he came to her. Their bodies twined together even as their tongues played and teased, kissing hotly, murmuring words of passion and need.

His teeth raked her nipples lightly through the camisole until the barrier become intolerable to them both. He pulled it off, less gently now, and suckled her urgently. Her fingers twined in his hair, holding him close, as pleasure coiled within her. When he eased the panties down her legs, she felt only relief.

"So beautiful," he murmured as he touched the soft nest of curls between her thighs. Her head fell back onto the pillow. His control was close to breaking, but he held on, determined to draw out her own release. When she finally could bear nothing more, he spread her legs and moved to enter her, but still he held back, waiting until her hand closed around him, guiding him to her.

Liz gasped at the hard fullness of him, but the shock faded almost instantly. He moved slowly, giving her time to adjust. Her hips lifted, matching his rhythm at first but then more quickly, urging him without words.

His last tenuous hold on control snapped. Hands grasping her buttocks, he lifted her to his thrusts, driving hard and deep until ecstasy shattered them both.

A long time afterward, when consciousness stirred, Liz opened her eyes. Deke lay beside her, his dark head close to her breasts. She touched his back gently, tenderness suffusing her. Close upon it came wonder. She had never felt such passion in her life, but neither had she ever behaved so impulsively. She felt almost as though she had become a stranger to herself. What if she had been wrong to trust him so utterly? What if she ended up regretting what had happened?

As though in response to her sudden fear, he lifted his head and looked at her. His eyes were infinitely gentle, but there was something else in them—his own apprehension.

"Regrets?" he asked.

Without hesitation, she shook her head. "No. You?"

"Well, there is the fact that I think I'm going to die. However, there's a lot to be said for going this way."

"Idiot," she said fondly and moved against him.

Apprehension vanished, to be replaced by surprise and that ever resilient male arrogance. "On second thought, maybe I'm not a goner yet."

"Maybe not."

"There might be a little life left."

"A little?"

"I'm being modest."

"Oh, I couldn't tell. Of course, if you'd rather rest . . ."

He growled and reached for her, drawing her away with him into the darkly whirling world of their own creation.

SIX

"Sweet," Liz murmured. She tipped her head back and let the mingled flavors of strawberry and chocolate trickle across her tongue.

They were lying in bed, propped up on fluffy feather pillows with a quilt thrown over them to ward off the late-evening chill. The strawberries were on a silver plate that curled around the edges and was engraved with clusters of grape vines. The silver had a fine patina of age, especially around the edges, suggesting that it had been sitting somewhere out of sight for a long time waiting to be rediscovered.

Deke had gone down to the kitchen to get the strawberries and returned with more of the crisp, cool Chablis. He sipped his wine, took another of the strawberries, and lifted the glass to her lips.

"Good?"

She savored it slowly and nodded. "Perfect."

She sighed deeply and stretched under the quilt. When had she last felt so content? Every particle of tension she had possessed was wrung out of her. Washington, D.C., the network, Hauster, her whole previous life, could have been part of a dream. This room, this man, seemed the only reality.

When the strawberries were gone, he set the silver plate on the floor and got up to close the curtains. "Will you stay?" he asked as he came back to the bed.

She looked up at him and hesitated. "I'm not used to this."

"I know. Neither am I." He sat down beside her and lifted the leaded crystal goblet that held his wine. It swirled pale gold in the soft light. He smiled and eased the quilt away from her breasts. When he touched his mouth to her nipple, she felt the coldness of the wine tart against her heated flesh.

"Stay," he murmured.

"Ever sell ice to Eskimos? I'll bet you'd be good at it."

He raised his head and smiled lazily. "This isn't that hard."

"Oh, now I'm easy."

"I didn't say that."

She made a soft sound and rubbed her fingers along his chin. "You're scratchy."

"I need a shave." He gave her a quick kiss, got off the bed, and disappeared in the direction of the bathroom.

Liz snuggled down under the covers for a few minutes before she gave in to temptation and followed him. He had left the door open and was standing at the sink, his face lathered and a razor in his hand. The mirror reflected his long, hard body bare of so much as a towel.

"Want to watch?" he asked, looking at her in the mirror. She followed his gaze and stood spellbound for a moment, caught by the differences between them. She had never thought of herself as delicate, but compared to him she looked like a supple reed that would bend easily before the wind. Her skin was paler except for the deep crimson of her nipples made all the more prominent by his attentions. Her hair was tousled, her lips swollen. She looked like exactly what she was—a woman who had been well and thoroughly loved.

Shyness almost drove her back, but before she could go, he put the razor down and took hold of her around the waist. Lifting her, he set her on the edge of the counter next to the sink.

"Keep me company," he said.

When he was done, they got into the shower together, standing under the steaming water as they soaped each other lingeringly. When they finally exhausted the possibilities that provided, Deke took a big white terry-cloth towel from the heated rack and dried her. He began with her hair and worked his way downward with commendable thoroughness. When her knees threatened to buckle, he lifted her and carried her back to the bed where they tumbled, exhausted, into dreamless sleep.

That began the pattern of their days. Deke worked while Liz finished the house and began to look around for other ways to occupy her time. She bought the material for a quilt and tried her hand at making applesauce. She also dodged Woodsleys with mixed success. Mostly, she just missed Deke.

In the evenings, they came together for dinner, conversation, and incandescent lovemaking. A week passed in a haze of pleasure-induced contentment. It ended the Saturday of the church social when they were sitting in the diner over burgers and malts.

It was raining outside. The gray clouds suited the grouchy little mood that had been trying to get hold of Liz ever since that morning when Vivian had called to report that things were pretty much the same as before.

"I hate to say it, kid," she told Liz, "but most people in this town are acting like they never heard of you. You've been erased from a thousand Rolodexes and then some. Hauster's riding higher than ever. He just announced a deal to build the world's tallest skyscraper in the middle of Manhattan.''

"Don't plan on renting space in it," Liz advised dryly. The fact that she had been effectively declared a nonperson didn't particularly concern her. Instead, she felt a sense of freedom she couldn't help but relish. As far as she was concerned, the whole world could forget she'd ever existed so long as that meant it would leave her alone.

"I'd love to chat," she said just a little deceitfully, "but I've got to go. There's a church social tonight and I'm on the decorating committee."

There was a satisfying inhalation of breath from way up in the big city and then, "You're what on the *what*?"

"Church social decorating committee, tonight."

"Look, are you all right?"

"Never better. Bye."

She hung up and made a halfhearted effort to restrain her laughter. Life did definitely go on.

She spent the morning working on the decorations, a task she'd been sideswiped into doing by Agnes, who really wouldn't take no for an answer. She and Vivian should have gotten together. They would have been dynamite. By lunchtime, she was famished and glad to be meeting Deke at the diner. Not even the knowing looks they got when they sat down at a booth together bothered her.

She was slathering ketchup on her burger when he leaned back against the cracked leather seat and without any warning said, "So have you about had it with doing nothing?"

She stopped in midslather and stared at him. "W-what?"

"This little vacation you've been on, I was just wondering if you were a little tired of it and maybe looking for something to do."

About halfway through the sentence, Deke started thinking maybe he should have phrased it differently. She was getting that glinty look in her eyes that he hadn't seen too often but knew meant nothing good. But what the heck, it wasn't as though he was some kind of insensitive macho stud. He was just trying to help her out. After all, she'd been dumped from a high-powered career. That had to be taking a toll. It was all well and good that she'd managed to keep herself busy so far, but how much longer would it be before she started getting bored when she was on her own? He was afraid of what that could mean and was determined to prevent it.

"I haven't exactly been doing nothing," Liz said with deceptive mildness. "I've cleaned my house from one end to the other, painted most of the rooms, polished the floors, started work on a quilt (she'd bought the material anyway), and learned to make applesauce *without* a microwave. I used to actually have nails with polish on them, but no more. And then there's all the exercise I've been getting at night, in case you've forgotten about that.''

"Whoa, I wasn't talking about us. All I meant was, if you want something to do during the day, you could come to work for WWDY.''

She knew about the station, having heard him mention it. She'd even tuned in long enough to figure out that he seemed to have a thing for Bette Davis. Now he was seriously talking about her *working* there?

"I don't think so," she said.

"Why not? The news end is pretty pathetic, frankly. You could punch it up.''

"You want me to do the news for WWDY?''

He nodded. "That's the idea.''

Liz had been about to spear a french fry with her fork. Instead, she put it down. It was either that or risk using the fork as a weapon.

"I had a thirty share on the network," she said slowly. "I interviewed the President of the United States—several times. I covered summits, for God's sake. And now you want me to read the hog prices on a local density station that reaches more trees than people?''

"Hey," Deke said, "there's no reason to get on your high horse. It was just a suggestion.''

"It was a lousy one.''

They sat in silence for several minutes before Liz sighed. Softly, she said, "Sorry.''

"It's okay.''

"No, I shouldn't have reacted like that. I was just surprised."

"You were offended."

"It wasn't that . . . All right, maybe it was. Vivian called this morning. She says I've been erased from everyone's Rolodex."

"Oh." He mulled that one over. On the surface it sounded sort of silly. But she did have a point. In a place like Washington, D.C., and especially in a world like television, who you knew and who knew you counted a lot. There would have been plenty of people only too happy to claim an acquaintanceship—or more—with Liz. But no more. Now all they wanted was to forget she'd ever existed.

"That's rough," he said, "but you're not really surprised, are you? You knew the score when you came up here or you wouldn't have left the city."

"I knew," Liz admitted. You didn't get shafted the way she had and survive. Still, it was tough to give up the last little fragment of hope. "I guess I just didn't quite believe."

"But now you do?"

"I don't have any choice."

"Then why don't you think about WWDY? At least it would get you back in front of a camera and you could call the shots so far as the news goes. It would keep your hand in."

"No."

"Just think about it."

"I have, and the answer's no."

He shook his head and went back to his burger, but he didn't look convinced. She had the idea she hadn't heard the last of this.

Later that evening, while she was waiting for him to pick her up, she wandered into the living room and flipped on the television. It had been years since she'd seen a black-and-white picture. Everything looked more dramatic, more finely etched, even the guy offering to paint your entire car for $59.95 any color, any way, in under one hour while you waited. If you acted right now, he'd throw in a paint job on your kid's bike for free.

Wondering if she'd be able to resist that, Liz spun the dial until Deke's face suddenly leaped out at her. He was wearing a jacket and tie, which caught her attention right away because she'd never seen him dressed like that before. Also, he was reading the news, really reading it from a piece of paper in his hand rather than a teleprompter.

"White House spokesperson Marvin Blackwater said today that the President's head cold is improving but he still remains on an abbreviated schedule. In the Middle East, reports of an impending peace settlement were denied by government representatives. The Dow Jones slipped thirty-seven points on rumors of increasing oil prices. On the local front, a bull got loose in Mac

Wiggins's pasture this afternoon and damaged several fruit trees before being recaptured. Also, let's not forget that there'll be square dancing and a bean supper at the church tonight to raise funds for the outreach programs. Tickets are ten dollars a head and if previous years are anything to go by, a good time will be had by all. That's it, folks. For those of you not heading to the social, one of the finest westerns ever made, *The Searchers* with John Wayne, airs next. Stay tuned.''

Another commercial came on, this one for a video rental store in Bradford. Liz flipped the TV off. She stared at the blank screen, shaking her head. That was it? That was the news? He'd been generous when he called it pathetic. Okay, he didn't have a lot of time to spend, not to mention money, but even so—

Not that it was any of her business. She had nothing to do with it. Besides, there were plenty of other ways for the citizens of Woodsley to find out what was going on in the world. They could read about it in the papers, although fewer and fewer people were bothering to do that these days. They could watch the news on the networks or on cable, except nobody had to tell her how superficial most of that was and how often the real significance of stories got lost in the rush to grab the highest ratings.

What did it matter anyway? People could get along without knowing what was going on in the

TUNE IN TOMORROW / 115

four corners of the earth, or in Washington, D.C., or the state capital, or down the road. They just couldn't function as responsible citizens of a democracy. Neither could they protect themselves from the sudden ups and downs, ins and outs, that could make life tough if they happened with no warning.

So what? Big deal. It wasn't her problem.

She was still telling herself that five minutes later when Deke drove up in the truck. He walked up the path, rang the bell, and waited while she answered. Liz's breath caught a little when she saw him. That was getting to be a habit lately, but she couldn't seem to help it. How did he manage to make a corduroy jacket, white shirt, undistinguished tie, and gray wool slacks look so good?

As it happened, Deke was thinking along the same lines. The white cotton dress she had on was Mexican, if he wasn't mistaken. She wore it off the shoulder with the swell of her breasts just visible, her hair down, and a good portion of her slender legs revealed by the flounced hem.

"Nice dress," he said, wondering exactly how long they had to stay at the social. The way he was feeling, about fifteen minutes would do it.

"You'd better wear a coat," he said. "It's a little chilly."

He helped her into it and took her arm as they walked back down the path. She could climb into the truck with no trouble, but he gave her a boost all the same with a hand to the derriere and grinned when she shot him a chiding look.

"You ever been to anything like this?" he asked when he'd gunned the motor.

"Back when I was a kid in Texas."

"Is that where you got that dress? It's very pretty, by the way."

The compliment warmed her. Considering that she'd heard far more flowery accolades from men who could have taken their sophistication and charm to the bank, she was surprised by her own reaction. But then, everything Deke did surprised her. Even after a week, she wasn't anywhere near used to the tender, fiery passion, the gentle humor, and the quiet at the center of his being where, more and more, she was finding her own peace.

"I got it across the border when I was on a trip back home a few years ago," she said. "I was kind of surprised I'd brought it up here, but then I packed in a hurry."

"I can imagine. By the way, I'm sorry I was a little late. There was more news this evening than usual."

"More news? That was more?"

The words were out before she could stop them. She glared at his grin.

"So you did watch," he said.

"I was flipping channels."

"Yeah, yeah. What did you think?"

"I agree with you, *The Searchers* is a great movie."

"No, I mean it, about the news."

Liz sighed. She been caught fair and square. Now she might as well get it over with. "You were right again, it's pathetic. However," she added quickly, "that does not mean I want anything to do with it."

"That's okay," he said, so soothingly that she was immediately suspicious.

"I mean it," she said.

"So do I. But maybe you could give me a few pointers, indicate where improvements might be made."

Liz could feel herself getting sucked in but couldn't figure out what to do about it. He'd read her right down the line. She was a professional, she had the training and the experience, and she couldn't stand to see a job done badly.

"It could be longer," she suggested grudgingly. "I realize you're dependent on the wire services, but you could add a little analysis."

"Like what?"

"Well, like tonight for instance. The President is out with a head cold? Come on, when's the last time that happened? When he had that surgery last year, he was back in the Oval Office two days later even though his doctors were telling him to take at least a week off. He's just not the kind to put himself on sick call, so either it's something a whole lot more serious or there's something else going on. It could tie in with the rumors coming out of the Mideast and those could be related to the price of oil rising. If there is a Mideast peace settlement in the works, the President would be up to his neck in last-minute negotiations and way too busy to stick to his usual schedule. But he wouldn't want to tip his hand because that could spook everyone and queer the deal. Also, peace would mean the oil-producing nations would have less need for income to buy weapons so they could curtail production. You see, it all ties together.''

Deke was staring at her oddly. The truck had stopped. They were at the church. People were streaming into the social hall next to it.

Liz noticed all this gradually. She was still caught up in the thrill of the hunt, tracing the elusive fact through the underbrush until *pay dirt!* a breaking story. She loved it, always had, and just then she would have given almost anything to be back in her old job, feeling the pulse and throb of history in the making.

Except she wasn't. She was in the truck with Deke, in Woodsley, Virginia, somewhere on the outer edge of the universe.

"I get a little carried away sometimes," she murmured.

"That was amazing," he said as he helped her down. "I would never have thought of that, but the way you explain it, it sounds as though it could actually be possible.''

"It doesn't matter. You shouldn't listen to me. WWDY is fine just the way it is.''

He opened the door to the social hall and stood aside for her to enter. Inside, a couple of banjo players were belting out a reel helped along by a fiddler and a fellow on accordion. The decorations Liz had helped put up earlier in the day were looking better than she remembered and the air was filling with the good smell of molasses and pork, popovers, and corn pudding. Added to that was the touch of Deke's hand at the small of her back, warm, secure, and somehow comforting.

For the edge of the universe, it wasn't bad.

Out of the corner of her eye, she caught a flash of red and saw Agnes bearing down on them.

"Come on," Liz said, gripping Deke's hand, "let's dance.''

They did through most of the evening and into the night as the old church hall rocked to laughter and good times. In between the doh-see-doh's and the promenades, Liz met more redheaded Woodsleys than she would have imagined could fit into a room together. They were all glad to know her but nobody pressed too hard, not even Agnes who just wanted to make sure they got double helpings on the corn pudding.

Finally, well past midnight, the music turned slow and soft, the high stepping petered out, and people started drifting off toward home. In the crisp clear darkness, there were calls of good night, admonitions to drive carefully, and promises to do it all again next year.

Liz snuggled in the truck, wrapped in her coat. She was pleasantly tired but still too excited to sleep. Maybe she'd had as good a time somewhere else but she sure couldn't remember it.

"That was fun," she said softly.

It was dark in the truck and darker still outside. She couldn't see Deke's face, but she could hear the smile in his voice. "Not too hard to take?"

"Not hard at all. Woodsley must be growing on me."

"Earlier tonight I wasn't sure. You sounded like you wished you could go back."

"I did, but it was just force of habit. There's nothing for me there."

Quietly, he said, "There is here."

Her hand reached out, lightly brushing his muscled thigh. She felt his strength and his certainty. A long sigh escaped her and she turned to reach for the car door handle.

SEVEN

"Would you like to come in?" Liz asked. They were standing on the porch; she had the key in her hand and she was feeling more self-conscious than she had since saying a grateful goodbye to adolescence.

They had already made love, for heaven's sake. What was she so nervous about?

She should be marveling at the luck that had suddenly produced him just when her life seemed to be taking the ultimate down-turn, not worrying over what it all meant and where it was going.

Her problem, she decided right then, was that she'd always been too much of a long-term person, always trying to figure out what the next year, the next decade, the next whatever would bring. She'd plotted her career step-by-step.

But this was different.

This was starlight and summer, sweet heat and sudden passion. Second thoughts simply weren't appropriate.

Deke put his hands in his pockets, shrugged his broad shoulders and said, "Sure."

Liz let her breath out slowly. Heck, if he could be that casual, so could she. "Fine," she said and turned around to unlock the door.

Which meant that she missed the quick tightening of his features, the sudden flare of light in his eyes, and the tender half-smile that flickered over his mouth.

She was—as more than a few of the Woodsleys would have said—a piece of work, was his Liz. His Liz.

He turned the words over his mind, liking the way they felt. She could be so cool and confident, yet she could turn shy on him in an instant just like she was doing now.

Not that he minded. What was happening between them knocked him more than a little off balance, too.

"Coffee would be nice," he suggested.

She complied, grateful to have something to do. He followed her into the kitchen and sat on one of the stools beside the counter.

Watching her as she moved around, putting water in the pot, spooning in the coffee, he asked, "Any more trouble with the bats?"

She shook her head. "Not a sign of them."

"How about moles?"

Her eyes narrowed. "Moles?"

He held up a hand with the thumb and index finger a few inches apart. "Little critters, long tails, dark brown. You could mistake them for mice but they're shaped differently. Seen any of them?"

"No. Am I likely to?"

"Probably not until winter. That's usually when they come inside."

"Oh, good," Liz murmured. "Anything else?"

"Raccoons," he suggested helpfully. "They like attics. Make sure yours stays sealed. The same for owls."

"Gotcha, keep the attic sealed and look out for moles." She plugged the coffee maker in and got a couple of cups from the cupboard.

"Of course, you'll get the odd skunk or two but that's nothing to worry about. Just a lot of stink and they go on about their business. They don't really like nesting around humans."

"Seems rather exclusionary of them," Liz murmured. "Cross off skunks."

"The woodchucks pretty well hibernate straight through, so do the foxes."

"Wise of them. Anything else?"

"Agnes saw one of those black bears last year, came down in early spring when the foraging in the hills had gotten scant. He didn't bother her any, but he did get a loaf cake she had on the windowsill.''

"I'm surprised he had the nerve. What about moose? Bobcat? Cougar? Grizzly? Anything in the elephant department?''

He grinned slowly. ''Not that I've heard about. Did see some tracks that could have been wolf but I wasn't sure.''

"You're making that up," she accused. "Trying to take advantage of the city girl.''

Deke's smile deepened. He got off the stool and came over to her, not touching but close enough so that she could feel his body heat.

"Now, that's the truth,'' he said, his voice soft and just slightly rough around the edges.

He looked down at her, watching the play of light in her hair and thought he'd never seen anything quite so lovely. Plenty of beautiful women had passed through his life but they'd all been brittle compared to Liz.

She was the real thing.

He ran a finger up her bare arm, savoring skin that felt like warm silk. Softly, he said, "I do like that dress.''

His hand curved around her shoulder and slipped down her back, massaging lightly.

Her head dropped back as pleasure coursed through her. "That feels good," she murmured.

Deke moved behind her. Gently, he pressed the muscles at the base of her neck, digging his thumbs in just enough to loosen them. "You're too tense," he said quietly.

"Force of habit."

"How so?"

Her head fell forward. A cascade of honey-hued hair hid her face. "Any new situation, I always react that way."

He lowered his head and touched his mouth gently to the vulnerable nape of her neck. She shivered against him. "This isn't completely new," he said.

"I know but it still feels as if it is. Everything is happening so suddenly."

His mouth stilled. Slowly, he raised his head. "It doesn't have to," he said. "That's up to you."

He meant it, Liz realized. Even though she could feel his arousal against the small of her back, he really meant what he said.

If she told him right then that she didn't want him to stay, he would go. Even more, she'd be willing to bet he wouldn't hold it against her.

Which was a far cry from some of the men she'd known in the Big City who, underneath those thousand dollar suits and hundred dollar haircuts, had about as much self-control as your average rhinoceros in heat.

But then Deke wasn't one of "the boys". He was an actual red-blooded, Grade A man.

"As it happens," she said, "there's something

to be said for not taking a lot of time to chew things over.''

He laughed deep in his chest. ''You're starting to sound like a country girl.''

''Yeah, well maybe I'm starting to think like one.''

She turned in his arms and touched a finger to his mouth. ''Any more critters I ought to know about?''

He caught her finger lightly between his teeth before releasing it. ''None that I can think of.''

''Oh, good. I thought maybe I'd concentrate on just one particular species to be found around here.''

His arms tightened around her, drawing her close. ''Which would that be?''

''Bet you can guess.'' Raising herself on tiptoe, she touched her mouth to his, slowly, savoring the taste and feel of him. Her tongue teased his lightly as her breasts pressed against his broad chest.

Deke stood perfectly still, letting her have her way, until it went about as far as he could stand. When that happened, his control didn't so much snap as it bent.

So did Liz as he cupped the back of her head, fingers tangling in her hair, and moved his mouth over hers with devastating thoroughness. As his tongue drove deep, claiming her sweet warmth, she moaned.

Her fingers dug into his back as she held onto

him, the only anchor in a world that was—so suddenly—slipping out of control.

He reached over and flicked off the coffee pot, then lifted her and strode toward the stairs. On the second floor, he found her room quickly and stepped inside.

There he set her down with careful gentleness as his hands went to the buttons of his shirt.

"You do something to me, Liz," he said, the words rough like velvet rubbed over granite. "I'm not sure what it is but I'm sure not about to argue with it."

"Very sensible of you," she murmured, her eyes on the broad expanse of muscled chest revealed as he stripped off the shirt and discarded it. He sat down to pull off his boots and smiled suddenly.

"When you were a kid, did you ever wonder about this?"

"Sure," Liz said, unabashedly watching him. In all her life, she had never seen anything more beautiful. His body was perfectly honed, long and hard yet with an intrinsic elegance as though he had been made with particular care.

Yet he was utterly unself-conscious in his grace as though all this—the passion, beauty, joy—were all perfectly natural without any of the contrivance others tried to put on it.

"I mean the clothes part," he said, standing again. "How people got out of them."

Her eyes widened slightly. As a matter of fact, she had wondered. "My chief concern was noses."

He laughed. "What to do with them while kissing?"

"Exactly."

"Let's find out," he suggested and reached for her.

Several minutes later, he looked up and said, "I think we've solved that problem."

Liz nodded. She didn't seen any reason just then to waste breath talking, especially when she had so little left.

The Mexican dress was hardly cumbersome but the touch of it against her skin was suddenly unbearable. She took a step back from him and slowly slid first one sleeve off and then the other.

Feeling his eyes on her, and glorying in them, she lowered the bodice. Beneath it she wore only a delicate strapless camisole trimmed with tiny rosebuds. The silk was almost sheer. She could feel it against her aroused nipples.

Deke drew his breath in. She was so lovely that she hardly seemed real. Aphrodite rising from the waves could not have been more beautiful.

The notion, so poetic and so at odds with his usual clear thinking, amused him. He smiled tenderly. "Let me help you."

"That's very nice of you," Liz said solemnly, "but I prefer to do this myself."

Deliberately, she raised one foot until it rested

on the edge of the bed. Slowly, she undid the strap of first one pump and then the next.

Removing them cost her several inches in height. More than ever, she was aware of the disparity in their sizes.

Though she was hardly a small women, Deke seemed to tower over her. He was all muscle and sinew, burnished skin, and stark male power.

Far from being intimidated by that, she felt strangely protected and free to give full rein to her deepest impulses.

As though she was completely alone, she wiggled out of the dress and let it fall in a pool of white froth around her feet. Below the camisole she wore a pair of lacy panties that left the taut skin of her belly bare.

Standing before him, she smiled. "I guess maybe I could use some help."

Deke was glad enough to oblige. Much more of this and he was likely to burst. But the instant he touched her, he felt unaccountably big and clumsy. Going very slowly, he tugged the silk ribbon at the top of the camisole until the bow came loose.

"Like this?" he asked huskily.

Liz nodded. Heat rushed through her. She had played this game just about as far as she could. The need for him was so great she doubted she could stand it much longer.

"Perfect," she whispered as the cool night air

touched her breasts. He slid the silk down over her hardened nipples, letting it linger just the tiniest moment on them before lowering it over her hips and down her thighs. Every touch of his hands sent new tremors racing through her.

She gasped when he suddenly dropped to one knee in front of her and touched the smooth skin of her abdomen with his mouth. His hands cupped her buttocks, holding her in place, as he traced the line of her panties with his tongue, teasing and provoking until she cried out.

"Deke, please . . ."

He stood, gathered her into his arms, and carried her to the bed. As she lay on the cool sheets, he came down beside her. His fingers edged under the elastic of the panties as he removed them.

"So beautiful," he said, his gaze raking over her. He ran his hands possessively from her slender feet up over her calves and thighs to the cluster of dark golden curls.

There he paused and straddled her, gently separating the soft flesh, touching and stroking her until her back arched and his name burst from her lips.

Quickly, he stepped away from the bed and stripped off his remaining clothes. Magnificently naked and fully aroused, he returned to her.

Liz gathered him close. The muscles of his back clenched as her hands stroked him, finding his narrow hips, drawing him to her. Yet still he held back, drawing out the anticipation to dizzying heights.

"Wait," he said huskily. Before she could protest, he turned her so that she lay face down on the bed. Never before had she realized how exquisitely sensitive her back was. The slightest touch of his mouth between her shoulder blades and along her spine made her shudder with pleasure.

She tried to turn back over but he held her implacably, bending her to his will in a way she had never guessed could so well suit her own.

There was an exquisite sense of helplessness in not being able to see him, not knowing where or how he would touch her next. Yet side-by-side with it was the overwhelming aura of protectiveness. He would never hurt her, she realized, but he would draw out her passion to an extent she had ever before even imagined was possible.

Slowly, his lips moved down her back to the dimple at the base of her spine. He laved it with his tongue as his hands squeezed her buttocks.

"You've got a great ass," he whispered roughly.

His hair-roughened thighs moved against hers. She could feel the heat pouring from him and smell the mingled scents of soap, leather and pure man that were intrinsically his own.

He raised her hips slightly and she felt his hand, stroking, delving, finding her most sensitive spot.

His thumb rubbed over it slowly, his touch light, perfectly gauged to her need.

The sounds she made were muted by the pillow but still distinct. She tried again to raise herself but succeeded only in pressing her buttocks more firmly against his erection.

The touch of him, hard against her, the terrible, driving need and the overwhelming sense of helplessness sent her over the edge. Waves of pleasure coursed through her as he held her, safe.

The tremors were just beginning to subside when he turned her over and gently brushed the hair away from her flushed face. Her eyes were dark with passion, her lips slightly swollen from the pressure of his kisses. The flush continued downward over her throat, spreading to the tips of her breasts.

He laid his palms over both, rotating them slowly. She gasped disbelievingly. Passion, sated just moments before, swept over her with unprecedented force. He raised himself above her, his need gloriously rampant.

"Take me," he said.

Liz stared at him as understanding dawned. He wanted to be sure—absolutely sure—that she had no doubts and above all, no regrets. Even having gone this far, whatever happened was by her choice.

From submissiveness to sudden control was a heady change. It sent her senses reeling but not so much so that she couldn't accept his offer. Or command. Or whatever it had been.

Her hand curled around the hard, thick length of him. From some inner depth of strength, she managed a smile.

"You're sure?" she whispered huskily. "I wouldn't want to take advantage." As she spoke, her fingers teased the smooth, swollen tip.

"Feel free," he instructed, his voice grating. At the limits of his control, he added, "But do it *now*."

Liz needed no further urging. She brought him close, close to the hot, moist craving waiting between her thighs . . . so very close.

A groan broke from him. He clasped her hips, lifted her, and thrust deep. Still holding her, he withdrew almost completely and plunged again. She cried out as her head tossed back and forth against the pillows.

Slowly, with enthralling care, he moved, drawing out her pleasure, heightening her need until the tension built to a crescendo. Then his control did at last break and he drove unhindered into her until the powerful, primal throbbing seized him.

Feeling it deep inside her tipped her over the edge, she joined him in explosive release.

They slept but woke again to moonlight pouring through the windows. Deke held her in the curve of his arm, slowly stroking her hair.

It was a moment of ephemeral beauty, sheer romance, delicately poised between reality and a dream.

Until his stomach rumbled. He looked sheepish.

Liz laughed. "Philistine."

"It has a mind of his own," he said apologetically.

She raised herself and looked down at him. They had kicked back the covers. He lay with one arm behind his head, unabashed in his nudity.

"Some part of you sure does," she said, "but I don't think it's your stomach."

He rolled his eyes in mock despair. "Isn't that just like a woman? Have her way with a man and then, when he's at his lowest, show no mercy."

Liz pretended to consider the merits of that. "Hmmm, it's a thought. However, I have a better idea."

"What?"

She leaned closer and said, slowly, savoring both syllables, "Brownies."

"You're a creature of sheer sensuality, woman. Brownies, really?"

She nodded and wiggled her eyebrows. "With nuts."

"I can't stand it." In a bound, he left the bed and tugged at her hand. "Let's go."

"Some poor male at his lowest," she grouched as he led her to the kitchen.

He opened the refrigerator, peered inside and

whistled. "Good God, you've got every convenience food known to man."

"I said I couldn't cook, not that I didn't eat."

The brownies were toward the back; she had some pride, after all. They took them back upstairs along with mugs of milk.

Sitting on the bed, they fed each other mouthfuls, licking their fingers and grinning unabashedly.

"You know," Liz said, "there are a lot of cultures where chocolate is considered an aphrodisiac."

"Really," Deke said, always willing to add to his store of knowledge. "Like where?"

"Like here," she said and set the empty plate on the table.

Pale silver bathed their bodies as they reached again for each other. Deke lay on his back as she moved above him, opulent in her nakedness, the epitome of all that was female. He held himself in strict check as she explored him with her mouth, her tongue, her hands, touching him every way and everywhere she would.

It became a contest between them—how long he could hold out, how swiftly she could provoke him. In such a competition, there were no losers.

Still, he was rather pleased with how long he managed until, at last, the roar of passion through his veins drowned out all other consideration.

He grasped her hips, maneuvering her until she was settled on the very tip of him. When she tried to move further, he forbid it, keeping her balanced just so until she cried out in protest.

Only then did he lower her slowly, inch by inch, until he was fully within her. She took hold of both his wrists and held his hands flat against the mattress.

It was a mock captivity, one he could easily break, but he indulged her and, in so doing, himself.

"My turn," she whispered in the night, on the scented air, as she began to move. The pace she set was slow, indulgent, even playful.

Until inevitably the play turned serious. Her inner muscles worked along the full length of him, drawing him deeper still. She arched her back, her head falling back. A vein throbbed against the whiteness of her throat.

The same pulse moved within him, encompassing them both, joining them as one.

A last, sweet thought followed him into sleep: his Liz.

EIGHT

The next day it rained. Not a little rain but a no-holds-barred downpour that sloshed in rivelets across the roads and turned the fields to instant mud.

Deke waded through it to check on the sheep. They were all doing well, including the new lambs. He'd left Liz's house (and bed) in the wee hours of the night, tearing himself away with palpable reluctance. Only the knowledge that another of the ewes was due and might be headed for trouble drove him back home. As it turned out, she'd beat him to the punch. The last of the season's get was already safe and snug in the straw.

As long as he was there, he thought he'd get caught up on some of the chores he'd been neglecting of late. He parceled out fodder, mucked out the stalls, and polished the tack. By the time he finished, it was midmorning and he was soaked through. He stripped off his clothes and climbed under the shower where he stood for a good fifteen minutes or so before feeling human again.

When he was dressed in dry clothes, he took a look out the window. The rain seemed worse than ever. He switched on the television and was surprised to see an unscheduled broadcast from Branford. Sam Wheeler was on the air telling people the storm was worsening. The local rivers and creeks were in danger of overflowing their banks.

Deke frowned. He didn't like the sound of that. The Maupeechuk River usually wound through town in a nice, picturesque fashion but occasionally it had been known to break loose and do some serious damage. It could be they were looking at another such occurrence real soon.

He decided to go see for himself but first he stopped by WWDY and picked up the minicam he'd treated himself to a year ago. He hadn't had much call to use it since fast-breaking news wasn't exactly a characteristic of backwoods Virginia life, but you never could tell.

The minicam fed directly to the satellite dish that squatted atop the roof of WWDY world headquarters. He made sure the link was up and running before he left, again just in case.

It was getting on toward noon by the time he headed toward town but the sky was so dark that it might have been late afternoon. Several times he had to slow down where the road was awash with water. Cascades of mud ran down the hillsides, making the going even tougher.

In town, he could see the lights on at the Pic & Save but it didn't look like anyone was shopping. Across the way at the Colony Diner, the story was different. There the parking lot was filled. That figured. Plenty of people remembered what had happened the last time the Maupeechuk flooded. There'd be a natural instinct to bond together in case help was needed.

Deke thought about joining the crowd, but first he took a swing past the river. Parked well out of reach, he watched the raging torrent of water where the normally placid current had been. Already it looked to be up a good four feet and the level was rising fast. He switched on the radio in time to hear a National Guard officer saying the area was under a flood warning and all emergency personnel should report for duty as ordered.

At one time, there had been a few houses along the banks of the Maupeechuk, but after a particularly severe series of floods in the 1950's, they'd been moved or abandoned. The only other structure that remained right close to the water was the bridge that linked the two sides of the main road running through town. It was a two-lane, wrought-iron span built early in the century and named for Nathan Daniel Woodsley, founder of the town.

There was a little plaque to that effect in the middle of it.

Deke walked across, noting as he did that the water rushing underneath was white-flecked and roiling. It looked like the ocean during a blow. He watched it whirl around the support struts for several minutes before returning to the truck.

The diner was a haven of warmth and light against the turmoil of the storm. He shook himself more or less dry and responded to the various greetings that came his way. Abby Woodsley was behind the counter; her husband, Bart, had come out of the kitchen in honor of the unusual circumstances and was chatting with a couple of truck drivers who had found it prudent to take shelter. Abby poured Deke a cup of coffee while he went to make a phone call.

The pay phone was down a narrow hall toward the rest rooms. He popped in a dime, punched Liz's number, and waited. It rang four times, five, six. Where was she? The house wasn't that big. Even if she'd decided to paint something (what was left?), she'd had plenty of time to get down off the ladder and answer the phone.

He stared at the opposite wall, past the anonymous numbers jotted down in pencil and the one nonanonymous suggestion that for a good time, it was wise to call Bruno. She couldn't have gone out, could she? The Jaquar was cute, but he'd never heard they were all that good in bad weather. She'd have had more sense, wouldn't she?

On second thought, maybe she wouldn't. He hung the phone up in disgust and went back to the counter. Abby had his coffee ready. She was a plumb, chatty woman who usually had a smile for everyone, but today she was looking grim.

"Getting pretty bad out there," she said.

Deke nodded absently. He glanced out the window. The sheets of rain were getting so thick it was impossible to see more than a few feet past them.

"Something wrong?" Abby asked.

"No, I don't think so. Are the phones working, as far as you know?"

"I guess. Granny George called a few minutes ago. She says the creek behind her house is running fierce."

"She need any help?"

"Tom and his boys are with her. She's fine. Everybody here knows the drill. Only ones we've got to worry about are strangers." She cast him a quick look. "You talk to Miss Sherwood?"

Deke shook his head. "There's no answer, but she's got to be there."

"I don't know. City girl like that might not know what can happen in a storm like this."

"She didn't always live in the city. She grew up in Texas."

Abby needed no explaining as to how he knew

this. Like everybody else around town, she took it for granted that there was a thing going on between Deke Adler and the TV woman. Even if she had been inclined to pursue the topic, she didn't get the chance. The door banged open on a rush of wind and a few more truckers clomped in. Abby was kept busy pouring coffee and taking orders. She was in the middle of telling Bart to rustle up a couple of meatloaf specials when she stopped all of a sudden, looking puzzled.

So did everybody else in the diner. Dead silence fell except for the sound that caused it, a queer, wrenching shriek like metal being twisted out of shape. It blocked out even the wind rattling the diner's windows and the lashing rain.

For several seconds, nobody moved. Deke was one of the first out of his seat and to the door. He flung it open and ran out into the storm. A gust of wind hit him hard and almost flung him back, but he stuck his head down and pushed on. He got as far as the other side of the parking lot right up near the road. There he stopped, staring in disbelief at the sight that greeted him.

The bridge was gone. Where it should have been there was only a twisted hunk of iron and a gaping hole with white water surging through it. A short distance downriver from the bridge, a small car bobbed helplessly in the rushing current.

There's one good thing to be said about a town like Woodsley: people were used to fending for themselves. Four of the men in the diner belonged to the volunteer fire department. They raced for their equipment while Bart Woodsley, who ran the paramedics, did the same. Abby took one look at the situation and hustled back inside to crank up the extra coffee urn. Three of the truckers grabbed chains they had in their rigs and followed Deke to the water's edge.

With some real luck, whoever had been in the car would have scrambled for safety before it went in. But luck wasn't running on the river that day. The men on the bank could see figures in the car— a man in the front, a woman beside him and in the back, pressed hard against the windows, two small children. They were all shouting frantically and pounding against the glass.

"Why don't they roll down the windows?" one of the truckers asked, his face tense with dread.

"Electric," Deke answered. "The battery would have shorted out when they went in. The doors will still unlock, at least until the water gets too deep, but the windows won't move. We've got to get to them fast."

Behind him, he could hear the wail of the fire truck approaching. The ambulance was close behind. For most emergencies, they would have been in good shape, but this was different. The car was too far away to be reached by the extension ladder. The current had lodged it against a clump of logs a hundred feet or so from the bridge. Given enough time, somebody could drive the five miles or so down the road to the next bridge, cross over, come up on the other side, walk along the bank, and get a chain attached to the car.

Except by the time anybody did that, the car would be gone and its occupants with it.

There was only one other solution, and as Deke stared at the darkly rushing water, he suspected who was going to have to take it. Back in high school he'd been on a swim team that took the state championship in large part due to his efforts. There'd been talk of his going for the Olympics. He hadn't done it because he'd always been too interested in other things to muster the single-minded dedication any such effort would have demanded. But he still swam every chance he got and thought of the water as his second home.

At least, until now. With a muttered curse, he started stripping off his rain gear.

Right about that time, Liz was deciding she'd made a mistake venturing out of the house. She would have stayed except being there on her own was getting on her nerves. Okay, it was raining hard, but so what?

So she could just barely see where she was going and the car kept sliding every which way all over the road, that's what. Deke had been right about her not being strictly a city girl, but in Abilene a serious rain meant a quarter-incher that raised more dust than anything else. This was a whole different kettle of fish. In fact, a whole school of fish could have survived quite happily in what was coming out of the sky. She was nuts not to just turn around and head for home except she was more than halfway to town, and on the twisty, turny road, turning around wasn't as easy as it sounded.

When she finally saw the roof of the Pic & Save straight ahead, she let out a sigh of relief. There were a bunch of cars at the diner. She'd pull in there, have a cup of coffee, maybe find out where Deke had gone to. She'd tried calling him, but there hadn't been any answer.

She was just making the right-hand turn into the parking lot when she saw the crowd gathered near the bridge. A fire truck was there along with an ambulance. She switched signals and kept going until dead ahead she could see where the road ran out.

No bridge. Just twisted metal and rushing water. If anyone had been on the span when it went, they'd have to be—

She slammed on the brakes, flipped the ignition, and jumped out of the car. The mackintosh she was wearing gave her some protection, but she could feel the sting of wet cold against the back. By this time there were several dozen people standing at the river's edge, all of them dressed pretty much as Liz was—except for the guy in the middle, who was bare-chested, wearing nothing but a pair of chinos, with a length of chain in his hands.

Liz's heart stopped. When it started up a second later, it hammered against her ribs so hard she could barely breath.

Please God, she prayed, *don't let this be. Don't let that be Deke looking for all the world as though he was about to plunge headfirst into the raging river with the chain, no less, weighing him down. Please, just don't.*

Then she saw the car.

Actually, what she really saw was the face of a child peering out the back windshield. The child's mouth was moving, but it was impossible to hear what she was saying. It looked as though she was crying.

"What happened?" she asked, to no one in particular. Abby heard her. She took one look at the pale face and the horror-filled eyes and put a capable arm around Liz's shoulders.

"Bridge went out," she said succinctly. "Come on over here and help me pour coffee."

It was a sensible instruction, intended to keep Liz busy while also getting her away from where she could see Deke directly. It was also well meant, for Abby was a kind woman who didn't need everything spelled out for her.

All the same, it didn't work.

Liz didn't mean to be rude, the thought would

never have occurred to her, but she was driven by forces that really were beyond her control. She wrenched herself away and ran to Deke, not caring who saw or heard.

"What are you doing?" she shouted above the roar of the water and the frantic noises of the crowd. "There has to be another way!"

He turned to her, his hair slicked down by rain that ran in rivelets over his bare skin. His eyes were filled with regret that she was here and, seeing this but also with relief for the sight of her, hard though it was, filled him with strength.

He dropped the chain and took her into his arms. She clung to him, heedless of the crowd, and felt the cold wetness of his skin mingling with her tears.

"There isn't any other," he said gently. "There's no time. Look, it's okay, I'm a good swimmer."

There was so much she could have said right then—that he was crazy, that no one could survive what he was planning, that his own life was too important to risk this way. But one look at the quiet, implacable strength in his face stopped her. That and the image of the child crying out for help.

"Oh, God," she whispered against his skin. "I don't want to lose you."

He smiled gently and touched her cheek, brushing away tears. "Same here. It's going to be fine. Do me a favor?"

A favor? She would have promised him the earth, the stars, and anything in between. But what he wanted was closer within her reach.

"There's a minicam in the cab of my truck. Like it or not, this is the biggest story to hit Woodsley in a hell of a long time. I can't get it on the air, but you can."

"No!" she protested, horrified that he would think her capable of treating the situation as a news story when he was risking his life.

"I want you to," he insisted. "Think about it. If this doesn't work and those people die, their relatives will be better off knowing we really tried to save them. Also, we've been trying for five years to get the state to upgrade this bridge. This is the most graphic evidence possible that they should have listened."

"You don't realize what you're asking," she said brokenly.

His look was infinitely tender. "Don't I? You're the best, Liz, you always were. I know you can do this."

She stared into his eyes, seeing the trust he had in her, and felt her resistence ebbing.

A big man with a heavy beard appeared beside them. He glanced from one to other. Almost apologetically, he said, "It's ready."

The various lengths of chain the truckers had with them had been linked together to form a single length several hundred feet long. Now all that remained was to get one end of it to the car and secure the vehicle before it could be dragged farther down the river.

Deke took hold of the chain. He stepped closer to the edge of the bank and stared down at the water. If anything, it was running faster than ever. He'd have all he could do and then some to stay afloat even without the weight of the chain. With it, he might easily drown.

To hell with that. He had too much to live for. He took one more look at Liz, filled his lungs, and jumped. The dive he made was perfect. It cut the air in a long, graceful arc. He entered the water with hardly a splash and disappeared from sight. The chain followed, pulled by his weight. Men on the bank rushed to secure the other end while others watched, waiting to see Deke break to the surface. Long moments passed before his dark head suddenly shone above the gray water.

Liz let out a sob of relief and ran for the truck. She found the minicam right where he said it would be. Automatically, she checked the link and hoisted the camera to her shoulder. The signal to the dish would be set to override anything the station was showing. Willing herself to sound as calm as possible, she switched the power on.

"This is Liz Sherwood for WWDY news. Regular programming is interrupted for this special bulletin. Woodsley Bridge over the Maupeechuk

River has been washed out by the storm. A car with passengers aboard has gone into the water. This is a live shot of the rescue effort that is underway.''

She panned down the river and through the viewer saw Deke being pulled along by the raging current. His head was still above water, but as she watched he went under, only to appear again a moment later.

Her heart in her throat, she said, ''Deke Adler, a resident of Woodsley and the owner of WWDY, is trying to reach the car to secure it so that the passengers can be removed.'' On the bank, the crowd was lined up in a row, holding fast to the chain and straining with all their might to see Deke. The viewer made the scene look small and far away. She hit the focus and zeroed in on the face of one of the truckers, his eyes locked on the bobbing figure being tossed so helplessly by the torrent. The man's lips could be seen to move as though in prayer.

''The emergency began just a few minutes ago,'' Liz went on, forcing herself to speak. ''Fire and ambulance personnel are on the scene.'' She panned again to show the scope of the effort and then zeroed in on the river. Deke was nearing the car, but the current threatened to pull him right by it. He would need all his strength to grab hold.

In the water, buffeted by the raging current, Deke fought to do just that. The effort was even harder than he'd expected. Large chunks of wood and other debris slammed into him. The chain kept threatening to pull him under and he could barely make out his goal through the raging white water and rain.

But he did see it finally and, gathering all his strength, he struck out. The current fought him every inch. His muscles burned and his lungs screamed for relief, but he kept going, slowly, laboriously, until at last his hand closed on the handle of a door. Immediately on the other side, a woman stared at him with mingled disbelief and terror. She started to reach her own hand down as though to open the door on her side, but Deke shouted at her not to do it—not yet. The moment the door opened, water would rush into the car. Its precariously balanced weight would be unsettled and it would be washed away.

He gestured to her to get down. As she huddled in the seat, he took the end of the chain, threw it back, and swung it directly at the car window. The glass did not break, but it did dissolve into a web of cracks. Cautiously, Deke pressed against it until a hole opened in the window. He passed the chain through. The man in the driver's seat grabbed it and followed what Deke had done and broke through the other window. The simplest thing then would have been to secure the chain across the roof of the car, but Deke didn't trust that. He knew most car roofs weren't sufficiently well made to take the kind of force that would be exerted by the raging river. The roof could easily be ripped off and the car lost. Instead, he had to go under.

He took a deep breath, ignored the pain raging through him, and dove. Beneath the surface, the water seemed calmer, but the impression was deceptive. The current ran every bit as strong. The car straddled two submerged trees front and back that had blocked its progress down the river. Without them, there would have been no chance at all. Swimming between the trees, Deke surfaced on the other side. Red spots floated before his eyes. He filled his starved lungs, grasped the end of the chain, and dove again. A minute passed and another before at long last he snapped the chain shut on itself, securing it with a steel padlock.

His strength gone, he clung to the chain as the river tore at him. An immense wave of sound pressed down from above. He raised his head, blinked to clear his vision, and saw the National Guard helicopter swooping down on them. Through the exhaustion and the pain, one thought filled him: he would see Liz again, he would hold her and touch her. Come hell or high water—he even smiled at that—he would make her his.

NINE

Deke drifted in a sea of contentment. Every inch of his body hurt, but that didn't matter. It was only welcome evidence that he was alive. Besides, beyond the pain, almost as a wall separating him from it, was pleasure so exquisite that he could have died from it and not minded.

He was lying in his own bed, listening to the rain fall far more softly now against the windows. Liz moved around the room quietly, shutting the curtains and easing the quilt up over him.

She had brought him home in the truck at his own insistence after he refused to go to the hospital. His ribs were bandaged, he was black and blue from one end to the other, and there was an ugly gash across his forehead, but she thought him the most beautiful thing she had ever seen. Even now she kept darting quick little glances at him just to be sure he was still there, alive and breathing, within reach of her hand.

The way she saw it, she'd probably taken ten years off her life standing there on the riverbank with the damn camera going waiting to see whether or not he was going to come back to her. When the helicopter plucked him and the rescued family out of the water, she hadn't known whether to cheer or cry. In the end, she'd done neither.

Instead, she'd gone to work, propping the camera up under the shelter of a tarp and using it to do interviews with the Guardsmen and others on the scene. She'd even interviewed Deke while the doctor was bandaging him. She'd done her job and she'd done it well. The live feed to WWDY was picked up by the Branford station, as per a standing agreement with Deke. They, in turn, fed it to their network. Not the one Liz had worked for, but another that she'd always considered a rival. The story would have merited putting on the evening news all on its own, but when the network realized who the blonde doing the interviewing was, they went full tilt.

Liz and her minicam got six minutes, no interruptions. When it was over, the anchorman, who looked like a close cousin of Tom Wilcox, smiled into the camera and said, "Many of us in television have been wondering lately what happened to Liz Sherwood. Now we know. She's alive and well in Virginia and still beating the best of the best to the punch. Nice work, Liz.''

As accolades went, it wasn't bad, but it did little to ease her mood. She couldn't sit still, couldn't think, couldn't relax. All she could do was keep remembering how close Deke had come to getting killed and how terrified that had made her feel.

She hadn't been that scared the time in Lebanon when she came under fire from one or the other of the factions tearing that poor country apart. Crouched against a wall, listening to the bullets whizzing by, she hadn't felt nearly as mortal as she did right now, safe and snug in the Virginia backwoods with hardly a care to call her own.

She had never felt so vulnerable in her life and she didn't like it. Damn the man. He had no right to do this to her. She'd been getting along just fine. Okay, she'd lost her job and her life was in ruins, but, aside from that, it hadn't been so bad. And then along he came, flaunting that drop-dead smile and luring her out of her carefully maintained shell.

Look where it got her. She was a nervous wreck. She'd started biting her nails again, for the first time in almost twenty years, and she kept thinking she was going to burst into tears at any moment.

She was in love.

Oh, no, not that! Crazy thought, forget it, X it right out. Not true, not her. Not him. No way, no how.

No doubt.

The nerve of the man, doing this to her. He could have been killed. He could have left her. He had no right.

"Damn you," she said.

Deke's eyes crept open. That was the best he could do at the moment. He stared at her in bewilderment.

"What did you say?" Actually, it sounded more like "Wha' d'ja sayh?" He was too tired to speak clearly and besides, his jaw hurt right along with the rest of him.

She came over to the bed, hands on her hips, wearing nothing more than one of the old white shirts left over from his Wall Street days. Beneath it she was naked, having treated herself to a shower after getting him into bed. Her hair tumbled around her shoulders. Her eyes didn't look cornflower-blue anymore. They were closer to the color of the sky on a hot, airless day when the temperature is up over a hundred and the sun shines with a head-throbbing glare.

"I said 'damn you'. What you did for that family was wonderful, but why do I have to feel about you the way I do?"

Generally speaking, Deke wasn't up to a lot of

chitchat right then, but for this question he was willing to make an exception.

"How's that?" he asked, and tried not to grin. It was liable to get her mad and, besides, it made his face feel like it was going to crack.

She shouldn't have started this. He was a hero, not the phony kind that were always getting invented for one reason or another, but the real thing. He deserved better.

"Forget it. I shouldn't have said anything. Go to sleep."

"Wait a sec. You can't just drop somethin' like tha' an' 'spect me to go to sleep. This was just gettin' interestin'."

"Just? What was the rest of the day, boring?"

"It was . . . strange. I never did anythin' like tha' 'fore."

A smile quivered at the edges of her mouth, but she repressed it determinedly. This was no time to start with him. "You can't talk. Go to sleep."

His fingers curled around hers. "Stay?"

She swallowed against the lump in her throat. "Do I look like I'm leaving?"

He started to shake his head, winced at the pain, and said, "No, you look good. Real good."

"You're incorrigible. There's not a spot on you that isn't bruised and battered. You need to sleep."

"Yes, there is. Want to see?"

"No! If you don't go to sleep, I will leave."

"Fibber. You can't."

"Why not?" she demanded.

"Because," he murmured, his voice fading, "I'm holdin' on t'you."

And he did. Even as he drifted into unconsciousness, his fingers remained firmly around hers. She could have pried them loose, but the effort didn't seem worthwhile. With a soft sigh, she slipped into the bed beside him. Deke shifted slightly. Without waking, he drew her into the curve of his body.

"I'm not eighteen anymore," Deke said. He sounded surprised by the discovery.

Beside him, Liz laughed. "No kidding? You just woke up this morning and realized that?"

He nodded. "It must have sneaked up on me when I wasn't paying attention." He grimaced as he tried to pull himself upright in the bed. Given the state of his body, that was futile. The sheer relief at being alive had given way to the reality of the situation; he was no kid anymore and the battering he'd taken the previous day was costing him plenty.

"I've got to get up," he said. "It's after six. The sheep need milking, the churners got to be checked, there's a dozen things to do."

"Tell me," Liz said. She'd anticipated this and was already dressed in jeans and a plaid shirt with her hair tied back out of the way. Much as she hated to wake him, she'd known she needed instructions so she brought him a nice hot cup of coffee and called his name softly until he opened his eyes. She hadn't counted on him trying to get out of bed and do it all himself but she should have. He was that kind of stubborn.

"You're not going anywhere," she said firmly. "I'm taking care of things for a while. Now drink your coffee and tell me what to do."

Deke looked at her dubiously. He vaguely remembered sleeping all night with her close by in his arms. Several times he'd surfaced from dreams of people screaming and water engulfing him, but the feel of her soft warmth had kept the terror at bay. Now she looked so scrubbed-clean good that he wanted to invite her back into bed with him. Except there wouldn't have been any point. As he'd said, he wasn't eighteen anymore.

"I don't like this," he said. "It's hard work and you could get hurt. I'm going to call up Bart and some of the other guys. They'll come over and do it."

"They've got their own problems," Liz said firmly. "The diner's basement is flooded and a couple of the roads are still washed out. Besides, what's the trick to milking a few sheep?"

"No trick," he admitted. "You just have to get them to settle down and trust you. The actual milking's done by machine. All you have to do is set things up."

"Fine. What about feeding them?"

He ran her through the list reluctantly. They were tasks he'd done every day for the past several years and he could do them with his eyes closed. But this was different. She'd never done such work in her life and he was genuinely worried about her.

"Be careful," he ordered as she was leaving the bedroom. "Most accidents on farms happen around machinery so if you get down to it and realize you're not absolutely sure what goes where, do nothing. Got that?

"Got it." She gave him a little wave and disappeared out the door, eager to get started.

Deke lay back on the bed and told himself he had nothing to worry about. She was a smart woman; she'd be fine. Besides, he had no choice. For once in his life he had to depend on somebody else. That it was Liz only made it tougher. He smiled despite himself. He was the one used to being in control, the strong, capable man others looked to for help. But at the moment, he was weak as a kitten. It was a humbling experience. He wanted to be able to do something about it, but he couldn't. All he could do was lie there and think about how what he'd just about convinced himself he was going to have to do without suddenly seemed within actual reach. He smiled again, and this time it didn't hurt at all.

*   *   *

It was nice that Deke was feeling better, but Liz didn't share the sentiment. At the moment, she was down on her hands and knees in wet straw trying to convince an ornery ewe to step up to the milking machine. You'd have thought this particular sheep had never heard of such a thing the way she was acting. Certainly she wasn't about to let anyone inflict such an indignity on her.

Liz pushed, the ewe stood. Liz pulled, the ewe balked. Head-to-head, eye-to-eye, Liz glared. "Mutton chops," she said. "Stew. Maybe a nice sheepskin jacket. Any of that appeal to you, you damn animal?"

The sheep thought it over. She tossed her head, rolled her eyes, and stepped up to the machine.

Liz let out a sigh of relief. Okay, she'd gotten the knack now. Deke had omitted telling her it took threats to make the system work. She went over to the next ewe, smiled and said, "Lanolin."

No trouble with that one at all. She was doing great until she hit number six. She let Liz get within a foot of her before she dealt a sharp kick with her hind legs. The ewe was quick, but Liz was no slouch herself, and she easily dodged out of the way. The blow missed, but that didn't save her from slipping on the damp straw and going down hard. She came up cursing. The ewe couldn't really be smiling, could she?

"Let me clarify something," Liz said. "I'm the human, I'm in charge. If I have to, I'll do this by hand, but I have very cold fingers and I don't think you'll like it.''

Maybe the ewe figured her point was made or maybe it was just a coincidence. Whichever, she didn't try anything more.

"So far, so good," Liz muttered. Despite the coolness in the barn, she was hot and itchy. Straw clung to her hair, her clothes, even her shoes. There was a good reason for that last part. Sheep had been doing what sheep do.

With the milking finally done, Liz set to mucking out the stalls. The ewes watched her benignly. By the time she had finished, her back ached, her shoulders throbbed, and she had remembered every use for deceased sheep that she'd ever heard of.

Next, she forked fresh hay into the stalls. That looked simple enough, but the first pitchforkfuls went sailing over her head, scattering into the farthest reaches of the barn. She tried again and slowly got the hang of it, but by the time she was done, she was breathing hard.

That left only the water troughs to fill. A kid could do that, right? Maybe so, but the hose got away from Liz, spraying her from head to toe before she managed to get hold of it again. There were people in Washington, D.C., who had always thought of Liz as very much a lady—a tough customer but still a lady—who would have been real surprised to hear the interesting words she knew. But the sheep didn't seem to care at all.

She was filthy dirty, soaking wet, and exhausted, but the milking was done and the sheep seen to. That left the horses. She decided she'd better tackle them while she still had some strength left. Compared to the sheep, the horses were the height of courtesy and cooperation. However, they were also bigger, which meant they needed more feed and water, and correspondingly, more mucking.

"Big deal," she said as the horses perked up their ears to listen. "I've been shoveling this stuff for years every time I went into a meeting with the Big Boys. At least it grows roses."

She carted out the last wheelbarrowful and forced herself to keep moving. If she stopped now, she'd be done for. The milk was in the churner when the very last little bit of her energy ran out. Sitting on the floor right there next to the wood fire, she put her head back against a pile of logs and closed her eyes. The small building was warm and snug, and the air was scented with the clean, sweet scent of milk. Who could ask for anything more?

Deke could. He was lying up in the bedroom, looking at the clock and getting nervous. She'd been gone too long. He never should have let her go off on her own. If anything happened to her, he'd never forgive himself. Here he was a grown man, lying in bed like some invalid while a woman did all the work. He must have been out of his mind to agree to that.

He sat up abruptly, pushed the covers back, and swung his legs over the edge. Bad move. His body shrieked, the throbbing around his ribs got suddenly worse, and his head swam. Too bad. He wasn't giving up now. Before he could think about it too much—or at all—he stood up. The good news was that the floor didn't rush to meet him. The bad news was that he almost wished it was.

Definitely not eighteen anymore. Slowly, one hand holding his ribs, he made his way across the room and pulled clothes out of the closet. Getting dressed was torture. There's no point dwelling on it, suffice it to say he managed it finally. By the time he did, the pain was easing some or maybe he was just turning numb. Whatever the case, he was grateful.

He made his way down the stairs gingerly and opened the front door. The rain had stopped but the sky was still overcast.

"Liz," he called.

No answer. He could hear the freshening breeze in the trees and far off toward the road, the sound of a car passing, but nothing else.

"Liz!" Louder this time and more urgent. Still nothing.

Once he got off the porch and started heading

across the yard, there was nothing to hold on to. He had to go even more carefully, but he finally made it to the barn and went inside. In the dim light, everything looked exactly as it should. The sheep glanced at him disinterestedly. There was fresh hay and water, the stalls were clean, everything perfect.

But still no sign of Liz. It was the same in the stables. Obviously she'd been there and she'd done a great job. He was starting to feel foolish for having worried about her when he got to the cheese house. It looked fine, too, except for the disheveled figure sitting on the floor, eyeing him dubiously.

"Let me make sure I've got this straight," Liz said. "You do this for fun?"

"Not exactly." He sat down beside her and tried not to let his relief show too much. On the one hand, she was okay. On the other, she didn't think what he normally did was a piece of cake. He would have felt a bit deflated if she'd come through without drawing a breath.

"There's a lot of satisfaction in working with nature," he said, "instead of against it. The fun comes when it's done and you see what you've accomplished."

"I'll have to take your word for that," she said ruefully. "What are you doing out of bed?"

"I got worried about you."

"You should have been worried about the sheep."

"They gave you trouble?"

"Oh, no, not at all. We got along just fine after I suggested they'd be happier as mutton stew."

"Great. Now their feelings will be hurt and I'll have to buy them something nice to make up for it."

She shot him a glinty stare. "You can be really strange sometimes, you know that?"

"Strangely wonderful? Strangely terrific? Or both?"

She laughed despite herself, but she turned serious when she said, "You really shouldn't be here. Those ribs are nothing to kid with. Let's get you back inside."

"Let's get both of us there," he said as he stood up and held out a hand to help her. Arms around each other's waists, they walked back to the house.

TEN

"To tell you the truth," Liz said, "it's a relief to be out from under that quilt."

Deke's brow furrowed. He was behind the wheel of the truck. It was a week after the bridge incident. Most of the bruises had healed and he was back to his old self.

"What quilt?" he asked. "The one on the bed?"

"No, the one I thought I'd make. I bought the material and I started cutting it out, but then when I realized what I'd actually have to do, I got overwhelmed. Same with the apples."

He chuckled. "Let me guess. You got carried away making applesauce?"

"How did you know?" she asked. She'd hidden all the evidence before he could see it, which wasn't easy when you considered how much space three dozen quarts of applesauce and four bushels of applesauce-to-be actually took up.

"Everybody does it," he replied. "It goes with being in the country. People come here and decide they're going to do all the domestic stuff they've never had a chance to do before. For instance, I took up carpentry."

"Did you make anything?"

"One of the worst-looking bookcases you'll ever see. It's down in the basement somewhere. By the time I got it done, I'd realized that running the farm was a full-time business, especially with WWDY thrown in. Speaking of which, are you sure about this?"

"No, but I figured what the heck."

"It's nice to find such enthusiasm in a fellow worker."

She noticed he was careful not to say employee. The deal they'd struck was that she would help out around the news end of WWDY in return for Deke's help fixing up her house. The inside painting was done, but the outside remained, along with the sagging steps, drooping gutters, and a bunch of other things she couldn't tackle on her own. They both knew he would have done the work for her whether she went with WWDY or not but that didn't matter.

"The way this works," Deke explained a short time later when they arrived at their destination, "is I subscribe to the wire services, plus there's a call-up service for the major newspapers. On local stories, people know to check in with the answering machine or drop me a note. We broadcast from six A.M. until eleven P.M. most days, sometimes with a late news broadcast thrown in. The regular news is at noon and six P.M. Most of the time the station runs preprogrammed, syndicated series, old movies, that kind of thing. We average eight minutes of commercials per hour."

"That many?" Liz said, surprised.

He shrugged. "I keep the rates low, and lately we've been getting more viewers. Also, I think businesses have cottoned to the fact that they can use a station like this to pinpoint advertising exactly where they want it."

"I guess so," Liz said. In the rarified realms of the network, she hadn't paid much attention to local stations much less to the low-density operations like WWDY, but maybe it was time to take another look. The way it sounded, if there hadn't already been such an operation in Woodsley, she might have been tempted to start one herself.

While Deke took care of paperwork, Liz got ready for her first scheduled news broadcast. The wires had a lot to say about the new Middle East peace initiative that was underway. She'd been right to see that coming. The Secretary of State was flying back and forth, cautious optimism was being expressed, who knew what might happen?

She put together the major international and national stories and then turned her attention to local news. There the big item remained the destroyed Maupeechuk Bridge. It looked as though the legislature was going to come through with emergency funding for its replacement. Meanwhile, Bart Woodsley was branching out from the diner. He'd gotten a license to run a two-car ferry back and forth across the river and expected to have it operating within a month. Liz filed a follow-up note to do a special broadcast of the first crossing. She checked the forecast from the National Weather Service, jotted down what the Dow Jones was doing, and was just turning her attention to the sports when an item crossed the wires. Ron Hauster was looking to sell his casinos to "raise cash for new business opportunities". Yeah, right. Any cash Hauster got hold of would go to pay his creditors. She smiled grimly. It was starting just as she'd expected, but much good it did her.

Deke dropped by her desk a few minutes later as she was putting the finishing touches on her copy. "Anything interesting?" he asked.

She looked up into the face already so dearly familiar to her. She knew every contour of it, how his beard scratched in the morning, how he had a little mole right behind his right ear, how the hair at the nape of his neck curled when it was wet. And she knew far more, every inch of that proudly male body, all its passion, strength, and tenderness. She had sat across the breakfast table from him, lain safe in his arms, held him within her. She'd seen him overwhelmingly powerful and overwhelmed by exhaustion. She knew how he teased, how he provoked, and how he left her feeling utterly fulfilled. Beyond everything, she knew she loved him.

A smile flitted across her face. She shook her head. "Nothing special."

The Hauster story could rot for all she cared. It was old news. What counted was now.

At six P.M. on the dot, Liz checked her mike, looked into the camera, and said, "Good evening. This is Liz Sherwood with the news. Today in Washington, the President said—"

And so it went for the thirty minutes she and Deke had decided were called for given everything going on in the world, not to mention Woodsley itself. At the first break—for a message from George and Dan's Fencing Company—she took a sip of water, smoothed her blouse, and decided this wasn't so bad after all. Whether you were talking to twenty-five million people or twenty-five hundred, the job was basically the same. You told what was happening and you told it straight.

Twenty-nine minutes and thirty seconds from when she started, she put down her copy, smiled, and said, "That's it for this evening, folks. Don't forget to drop by the bake sale down at the school tomorrow. The money's for new computers. Have a good evening.''

"Nice job," Deke said when her mike was switched off. He came out of the control room smiling. "You looked like you were enjoying yourself."

"I was," she admitted. "You were right and I was wrong. I appreciate your convincing me to come around."

He sighed. "You're no fun. I was looking forward to dragging that out of you."

Liz stood up and came away from the desk. She stood very close to him, absently fingering the top button of her blouse.

"Oh, yeah?"

"Oh, yeah, what?" he asked.

"I'm no fun. How much you wanna bet?"

His eyes darkened as they swept over her. "I don't know. This sounds like 'heads I win, tails you lose.' "

"Something like that." Deliberately, she moved closer still. "What's playing this evening?"

"Six episodes of *The Dobie Gillis Show*."

"Rats. I love that show and here I was thinking maybe we could—"

"I'll tell you what," he said as his arms closed around her, "anytime you want, I'll arrange a private showing, but right now—"

"Hmm?" His lips touched her throat, trailing

fire. The gentle teasing dissolved, giving way to flaring passion.

"Right now," he said, "I've got something better in mind."

She looked at him in pretended shock. "You can't mean . . . here in the office?"

He laughed and lifted her so that her feet were left dangling off the floor and she was pressed firmly against his arousal. "It beats the truck."

Clinging to him, Liz gasped and felt the waves of need cresting within her. The game was fun, but the reality was vastly more. She couldn't resist him, couldn't even muster the will to try. The hunger between them was too raw and primitive for that.

The same thought gripped Deke. He cherished this woman, he wanted to treat her with consummate care, and he always had in all their lovemaking. But suddenly the heat in his blood was wild and savage, demanding immediate release.

In a corner of his office, near his battered old desk, was an equally battered old couch. He laid her on it and came down swiftly beside her. They strained toward each other, too anxious to undress fully. He raised her skirt, his hands slipping beneath to caress her urgently.

The swift firing of their passion astounded her. She had never felt anything like it. It was as though their bodies were now so well attuned to each other that they set their own pace with no thought to anything else. Slow seduction was out of the question. She reached down, undoing his pants, and gasped when she felt him. They came together in a single thrust. He moved above her, his face taut. Eyes locked on hers, he drew her higher and higher, holding back as long as he could until, so quickly, the passion burst upon them both and all restraint shattered.

Afterward, he cupped her face in the palm of his hand and said thickly, "God, Liz, I'm sorry."

She turned, her eyes still cloudy with pleasure. Her lips were swollen from the fierceness of his kisses. Deep within, her body still throbbed. His possession had been absolute. He had left her nothing and he had given her everything.

"Sorry?" she repeated, not understanding.

"I've never . . . that is, I wouldn't . . ." To her amazement, a dark flush suffused his cheeks. "Damn it, Liz, I've never done anything like that in my life. I could have hurt you. I could have—"

Swiftly, she touched her fingers to his lips, stilling him. "I've got a hot news flash for you. I was as much a party to what happened here as you. In fact, if I remember correctly, it was my idea."

"Yes, but—"

"No buts. You're a beautiful man. I can't keep my hands off you. Besides, I'm in love with you. But this couch is absolutely killing my back so if you don't mind—"

He moved just enough to let her sit up. His gaze was suddenly intent. "What did you say?"

"The couch. Don't get me wrong, I could develop a definite fondness for it, but—"

"Not that, the other."

"Oh, that. Well, you *are* beautiful. There are guys working out twenty hours a day for the body you got mucking stalls. Talk about life not being fair. Listen, I'm starving. Do you think we could get something to eat?"

He smiled indulgently and stayed right where he was. "I love you, too."

She stopped, her breath catching. "Oh."

"Oh, indeed."

They stared at each other. Liz started to smile. So did Deke. Relief was contagious, joy even more so.

"Gee whiz," she murmured.

"Holy smokes."

"I didn't think—"

"Neither did I, at first. But, hey, so you don't like bats. I can live with that."

Suddenly, Liz began to laugh. Deke looked at her quizzically. "What so funny?" he asked.

"I was just thinking, I should send Ron Hauster a thank-you note."

"Why not just make it an invitation?"

"Invitation? To what?"

"Uh, well, you know—"

When she didn't respond but just kept staring

at him, he cleared his throat. "Look, I know this is sudden, but we're not exactly kids and what we've got together is pretty rare. I think we ought to take advantage of it."

Liz's eyes widened. He didn't . . . he wasn't . . . He was! This was it. The Big Moment. The Whole Shebang. She wasn't ready, it was too soon. And what about romance? Their present position was certainly intimate, but it sure wasn't hearts and flowers.

"M— Uh, mar— You know, that, it's such a big step." Great, she couldn't even get the word out. Her heart was pounding, her throat was dry, and large sections of her brain seemed to be shutting down.

"That's true," Deke said gravely.

"M— Mar—"

"Marriage," he prompted, ever helpful.

"That, it's never really been in the game plan . . ."

"On the drawing board?"

She nodded. "In the cards."

"Up the sleeve?"

"Right. M— Marriage—" She'd said it! Funny, how that one little word could send bursts of heat curling right through her. "Marriage is such a big step."

"Absolutely, and we're both such sensible people."

Sheep doo, they were anything but. Her eyes

met his. Her heart was beating so hard, she was sure he could hear it. His hand rested on her bare thigh. She had only to move the smallest bit to feel the hard strength of him.

She cleared her throat. "Being sensible can be overrated."

He nodded solemnly. "That's true and it never kept anyone warm at night."

Or made for much of a life, either.

"We could throw caution to the wind," she suggested.

"Go for broke?"

"In for a penny . . ."

"In for a pound?"

She nodded and touched him gently, tracing the hard line of his mouth. "I meant what I said, I love you so much it scares me. Would you mind awfully if I thought this over a little?" It was her turn to flush. "I'm sort of discombobulated at the moment, you know?"

He glanced down, taking in their continued state of dishevelment, and nodded. Standing up, he straightened his own clothing and helped her to do the same.

"How much time do you think you'll need?" he asked, holding her gently.

"I don't know . . . I've never done this before. A couple of days?"

He smiled, relieved that she didn't think she

needed more. "You do understand that I reserve the right to persuade you?"

Her smile matched his own. "I can stand that."

He laughed, almost glad that she hadn't given him an answer right away. Everything had happened so quickly between them, what was the harm in drawing it out a little more?

Liz agreed. She was in love with a wonderful man, her life had taken a fantastic new turn, and ahead lay a future she could still hardly believe could be her own.

What could possibly go wrong?

In the back of her mind she could hear her mother saying, "Don't count your chickens before they hatch, Elizabeth Jane. A stitch in time saves nine, and while you're at it, don't tempt fate, not ever, because one'll get you two, you'll be sorry if you do."

Actually, her mother had never talked like that except way down in her own imagination among all the debris left over from childhood.

Who did talk like that, or close to it, was the very nervous bank president who right at that moment was getting down and dirty with Ron Hauster, something he had done his absolute damndest to avoid but which couldn't be put off a moment longer.

"I am afraid," the bank president was saying, "that we have a problem."

Hauster turned away from his perusal of the New York street scene, looked at the pinstriped codfish facing him and snarled, "*We*? *We* have a problem? Since when did you and me become partners?"

The banker frowned. He was finding this most distasteful. His palms were sweating and that ulcer he'd thought he kicked was definitely on the way back. Still, there were limits to what a man could be expected to stand for, and he'd just about reached his.

"Since the bank lent you something over a billion dollars, Mr. Hauster, a significant portion of which is now due and payable. Do I take it you are in a position to meet that obligation?"

Hauster hesitated. He wanted to tell the codfish to get out of his face. But that was one luxury he couldn't afford. After all the years and all the wild ride into the stratsophere of high-stakes finance, he'd finally found a game he couldn't rig. The truth of that was just starting to really sink in. It made him queasy.

"Yeah, well, you see," he said, "this is how it is."

ELEVEN

A bell was going off right next to Liz's ear. She tried to swat it away and, failing that, burrowed under the pillow, hoping to block it out. Nothing worked. The clanging went right on, dragging her from the well of sleep.

"Whazzit?" she mumbled into the receiver.

"Sweetheart! You're there, this is wonderful! I'm so glad I reached you. How *are* you? Great, of course. Isn't it the most fantastic thing?"

Liz put the receiver a few inches away from her ear and stared at it. Who was this person? The voice sounded familiar, but she couldn't for the life of her figure out what was being said.

Neither did she care. Deke stirred beside her and gave her a blurry-eyed smile. As well he should considering what he'd been up to all night.

When he said he reserved the right to persuade her, he wasn't kidding. Maybe she ought to stall a few more days just to see how long he could last. She smiled at the thought, ignoring the sounds that continued on down the phone line.

"Just fantastic . . . been on the phone for an hour with them . . . eating crow . . . incredible . . . you have to . . . right away . . . no time to lose . . ."

"Who's that?" Deke asked.

"Vivian, I think. I told you we should have gone to your place."

"Yours was closer," he pointed out, not unreasonably. "What does she want?"

"I don't know." She brought the receiver closer. "Vivian, what do you want?"

The voice went up another decibel. "What do I want? You've got to be kidding! I want you down here right away. We've got to strategize. We're gonna hold their feet to the fire like they've never been held. I can't wait! How fast can you get here?"

"Something's happened," Liz said to Deke. Talk about a shrewd observation. She'd never heard Vivian like this. The woman sounded positively giddy.

Deke shrugged and got out of the bed. He didn't want her to see his sudden apprehension. "I'm going to get shaved."

She watched him go, admiring the superbly

masculine grace of his body. When he disappeared into the bathroom, she sighed and turned back to the phone reluctantly.

"What was that?" she asked.

"What was what? Didn't you hear what I said? Hauster's gone belly up. He defaulted on almost a billion dollars in loans! The network's going nuts, they can't believe they axed you. They want you back, babe, all the way, bigger and better than ever. You can write your own ticket. The sky's the limit. This is gonna be the deal to end all deals." She paused a moment, for breath or for effect, then went in with the clincher. "They're talking anchor, honey, and they're serious. It's yours. All you have to do is say yes."

Liz lay back against the pillows, the phone in her hand, and shut her eyes tight. She couldn't believe this was happening. Sure, she'd predicted it, but she'd never expected Hauster to fall so hard or so fast. And she certainly hadn't expected it to have any effect on her. That part of her life was over and done with.

Wasn't it?

Nearby in the bathroom, she could hear water running. In the ordinary course of events, she'd be getting up about now to fix a pot of coffee. She and Deke would shower and dress and have breakfast, all the while sharing the tender looks and lingering touches of lovers. Beyond the bedroom windows the sky was bright, the last of the storm gone. It was a perfect day for being outside, working on a sagging porch, laughing together, planning a future.

Washington, D.C., the network, her career, were all a lifetime away. And yet, suddenly, they were all once again in the palm of her hand.

"Come back," Vivian said urgently. "This is everything you've been waiting for." Sensing hesitation, her voice took on an edge of disbelief. "For God's sake, Liz, this is where you belong."

Was it?

"I don't think so," she said.

Dead silence. Or maybe dead Vivian. The shock of that was enough to kill her.

Finally, in a hushed tone redolent of extreme disbelief, she said, "You're not serious."

It wasn't a question. In Vivian's universe, it simply was not possible that anyone would turn down a network anchor slot. Nobody, absolutely nobody with any claim to sanity, would walk away from a multimillion-dollar salary, genuine power, and a fistful of perks.

Liz sighed. She was sorry this was happening and she wanted to just end it, but she owed Vivian some explanation.

"Look," she said, "I've found something good here, something I really want. I know it's hard to believe, but the idea of going back just doesn't appeal to me. That part of my life is over."

Vivian thought about that for a moment.

"Good," she said. "Very good. I like it. Bring that attitude to the negotiations and we'll do even better than I was hoping. Look them straight in the eye, tell them you sincerely don't want to come back, and they'll cut their wrists open for you."

"Vivian, I'm serious! I like it here and I—"

"You *what*? You got dropped on your head? You can't seriously mean to turn your back on this! This is everything you've ever wanted. All you have to do is reach out and take it!" Sensing that she wasn't getting through, she moved in for the kill. "Besides, you have a responsibility to all the other women in television journalism. It's been an uphill battle for every one of you. How do you think it's going to look if a woman finally gets a shot at anchor and turns it down?"

"Don't pull that on me. If I don't get it, Connie will, or Jane, or somebody else, but it will happen. I'm not some damn Joan of Arc, and nobody's going to make me out that way."

"All right, all right, calm down. I've caught you at a bad time, obviously. You need to digest what's happened. Getting fired was a terrible trauma, I understand that. You've been through a bad time and you've been very brave, but sweetheart, it's over. You can have your life back better than ever. Don't say anything now," she added quickly, "just think about it, that's all I ask. And then call me. For God's sake, call me!"

The phone went dead. Liz put the receiver down. She could hear the shower running. She got out of bed slowly, put on a robe, and went downstairs. The kitchen looked warm and cheerful. Sunlight streamed in through the curtains she'd hung, and the freshly painted walls glowed brightly. She got the coffee going and sat at the table to wait for it.

That was where Deke found her when he came down a few minutes later. He had a towel around his waist and his hair was damp. He poured himself a cup and took the chair beside her.

"What's up?" he asked.

She took a deep breath, exhaling slowly, and shrugged. "Hauster's gone bankrupt."

Deke whistled softly. "How bad?"

"I don't know exactly, but it seems he defaulted on almost a billion in loans."

"So you were right."

"Seems that way." She got up to refill her cup. When she came back, he was looking at her strangely.

"I thought you'd be more excited," he said.

"About what? I knew Hauster was going under, it was just a question of when. This is no surprise."

"Maybe not, but there are implications—"

"Only for the folks who loaned him money. They'll be lucky to see ten cents on the dollar before this is over."

"That's not what I mean. The network fired you because of the Hauster story. Now it's clear to everyone that you were right. Surely, there's going to be some fallout from that?"

"So what? I've made my position plain. It's over and done with as far as I'm concerned."

"Is it?"

She turned her head away and stared unseeingly out the window. "You sound like Vivian. Why is it I can't get people to believe me?"

"Maybe because television and your career were your whole life before this happened," Deke said quietly.

She looked at him again, hard. "Before is the operative word. I've found something better." She reached out a hand, touching him. Her fingers trembled only slightly. "Deke, I love you. I want to stay here with you. I have absolutely no interest in going back to D.C.

How he wanted to believe her. It would be so simple, everything would fall into place. But doubt lingered. They'd had so little time together, and now this. What if she was mistaken? What if she stayed and came to regret it?

Quietly, he said, "Yesterday you weren't so sure."

"I was taken by surprise," she insisted. "No one's ever asked me to marry him before."

"You're kidding? Why not?"

She laughed faintly. What a question. "I guess

I was too busy and maybe I scared some men off, but you're the first one to suggest settling down, and certainly the only one I've ever wanted to do it with."

"But yesterday—"

"Forget yesterday! I love you."

"I love you, too," he said gently. Regret twisted through him. She was so beautiful, not just on the outside but inside where it really counted. She filled him with joy and made him believe in endless possibilities. But he couldn't be sure. She'd lost so much and now suddenly she was in a position to get it all back. How could she be so certain that didn't matter?

"You have to understand," he said quietly, "I saw firsthand a marriage that shouldn't have been. My parents lived with it for decades and it almost destroyed them, not to mention what it did to the rest of us. I can't take the risk of that. If we're to have anything together, I have to be sure that it's really what you want."

She drew back, staring at him across the expanse of the table. "Life doesn't come with any guarantees, Deke. You must know that."

He nodded. "I do, but I also know that you didn't choose to give up the life you had. That decision was forced on you. All I'm saying is that it should be a real choice. You need to take a look at all your options and then make an honest decision."

He meant it, she realized dazedly. He truly did want her to go even if that meant losing her forever. And he said he loved her? How could he really feel that way and still sit there so calmly, contemplating the possibility that she wouldn't return?

Maybe he was right, maybe it had all happened too fast.

The floor seemed to be falling out from under her. There was nothing left except hollow space. "All right," she said abruptly. "I'll go."

Deke's stomach twisted, but he said nothing. This was how it had to be. Never mind that he wanted to grab hold of her with all his strength and insist that she stay. She was everything he'd ever wanted in a woman and then some. He wanted to have children with her and grow old beside her.

No guarantees, she'd said, and she was right. Far from making any promises, life had a way of kicking you right in the head. Like now.

It was going to be a tough few days.

Deke left a short time later. They said very little more to each other for, after all, what was there to say? When he was gone, Liz tidied up the kitchen and went back upstairs. She made the bed by rote, refusing to think about the ecstasy they had shared there such a short time before. When that was done, she showered quickly, dried her hair, and walked over to her closet.

Way in the back, pushed well out of sight, were a handful of suits of the kind she was used to wearing every day. They were elegant, expensive, and in bright, feminine colors. Perfect for television.

She selected the first one her hand touched and put it on. After several weeks in jeans and sweaters, it felt strange to wear so many clothes. The shoes were the worst. She hadn't worn high heels since leaving New York and her feet would clearly just as soon have left it that way.

Limping slightly, she picked up her handbag and headed for the car. She'd call Vivian when she got to Washington, D.C. First, she had some hard thinking to do. But no crying, absolutely not. That stuff on her cheeks wasn't tears. The air was damp, that was all. Maybe it would rain again. That would suit her mood perfectly.

TWELVE

"The way we see it," Wheaton said, "we'd like to showcase Liz in a series of high-visibility specials in addition, of course, to her regular work as anchor of the nightly news. Naturally, the total package would reflect her broad range of responsibilities and her contribution across the board to the network's bottom line."

"The total package" was code for the dough, Liz's personal bottom line, which, if the tone of the meeting was anything to go by, was due to go through the roof. Or so Vivian thought. Looking sleek and predatory in a black sharkskin Ungaro suit, she nodded encouragement as Wheaton spoke.

They were sitting in the twenty-fifth-floor boardroom on the top of network headquarters in the center of Washington, D.C., with a fantastic view across the city to the rolling hills beyond. Liz was there, of course, along with Wheaton for the network, Daugherty for the news division (a very subdued and apologetic Daugherty to be sure), and Vivian, who was making no bones about the fact that she was having the time of her life.

"You realize," she said, hitching the nearly skintight skirt another inch up her shapely legs, "that when you canned Liz, you voided her contract? We're free to go anywhere."

Wheaton smiled. Actually, what he did was bare his teeth. Of all those in the room, he was the only one standing. While he talked, he paced back and forth between the windows with their panoramic view and the mahogany table where the others were sitting. He had his jacket off and was stripped down to a crisp white shirt, school tie, and charcoal-gray suit pants. This was supposed to show he was a regular guy, but Liz thought he looked anything but. He had the overly smooth, overly assured manner of those born to privilege who decide early on that they somehow deserve it.

Vivian smiled back. Unlike Liz, she thought Wheaton was attractive. In fact, she made a mental note that when this was all over, maybe they ought to get better acquainted. But first, business.

"I'm not kidding," she said. "We agreed to this meeting as a courtesy, but I'll be frank with you. Every major news operation you can name wants my client. Why, I ask you, should she return here where we have ample evidence that she was not appreciated?''

"Vivian, Vivian, Vivian," Wheaton said as though he was chanting a mantra, "don't you think we know how wrong we were?" He spread his hands and did a perfect imitation of man in the throes of contrition. "What can I say except that we made a terrible mistake. But to be honest, we had no idea of what we were up against. The disappearance of the evidence, the reluctance of witnesses to repeat what they had told Liz—'' He sighed as though bemoaning all the sorrows of the world. "What could we do? We felt we had no choice, although with hindsight, of course, we should have been totally supportive of Liz. No question about that.''

Vivian nodded, but Liz herself offered no response. She continued to stare off into space as though the discussion going on all around her really had nothing in particular to do with her.

Inevitably, her lack of involvement finally got through to the rest. Wheaton cleared his throat. "Uh, Liz, is something wrong?"

She looked at him blankly. "What? Oh, I'm sorry, no, everything's fine." She couldn't very well tell him that she'd been mentally back in a barn in Woodsley, Virginia, wondering if the sheep needed milking.

"That's just a general fine," Vivian said, jumping in. She shot her client a chiding glance as though to say let's not overdo it. Try to show at least a tiny bit of interest just so you don't put your foot in your mouth. "It doesn't mean that Liz thinks these terms are fine. There's still a great deal to discuss."

"Of course, of course," Wheaton said. He was one of those people who constantly and seemingly unconsciously repeated things, as though they deserved repetition. "What do you say we all have a nice lunch and relax, and then we can take up where we left off later."

"Lovely," Vivian said, unwinding herself from her chair. She stood up, took Wheaton's arm, and flashed Liz an encouraging grin. At least it was meant to be encouraging. Liz hardly noticed. Chances were she would have stayed right where she was if Daugherty hadn't cleared his throat to get her attention.

"Shall we?" he asked.

"Oh, sure." He took her arm, patting her hand a little clumsily, and led her next door to the private dining room kept for the exclusive use of board members and the highest ranking network executives. Liz had been in it only once before, at the annual dinner given by the network honchos for the top news correspondents. It had been a tiresome affair full of false cheer and strained efforts at camaraderie no one felt. For real newspeople like Liz—and Wilcox, too—management was automatically the enemy. Both sides knew that whether they wanted to admit it or not.

Whereas the boardroom was all somber mahogany, paneled walls, and oil paintings of former network presidents in heavy gilded frames, the dining room was strictly modern. An enormous slab of glass rested on a polished marble pedestal. Chrome-and-leather chairs that looked like they might be meant for aliens were collected around it. The floor was a mosaic of flames shooting off toward an unidentifiable target, unsoftened by anything so mundane as a rug. As it had the only other time she was there, the room made Liz think of an elaborate interrogation chamber in some twenty-first-century totalitarian state. Of course, she was far too polite to say so.

"Fantastic," Vivian said, glancing around. "Is that a Rheinstahsen?" She gestured toward a large canvas splashed with what looked to Liz like up-turned cans of paint poured indiscriminately across it.

"We bought before he was really hot," Wheaton said modestly.

"Brilliant," Vivian said. She and Wheaton stood for a moment, gazing reverently at the gaudy canvas.

It was left to Liz to break the mood. "Do you mind if we eat?" she asked.

The others looked startled. Quickly, Vivian said, "Liz, you're hungry. I'm so sorry, I should have realized. Ham, she's hungry.'' As though that explained her strange air of distraction.

"Here," Daugherty said, pulling out a chair, "sit down."

Liz did, mainly because she couldn't think of any reason not to. It was much simpler not to think at all.

People bustled around, white-jacketed waiters taking drink orders and proffering menus.

"So, Liz," Wheaton said when they had made their selections, "how was Virginia?"

Vivian shot him a glinty look. "All things considered, Ham, it may not be too diplomatic to bring up Virginia. Liz certainly didn't go there for the fun of it."

"Oh, gosh," Ham said, "I'm sorry. I just meant maybe a little break wasn't such a bad thing." He beamed her his sincere look. "You do work incredibly hard, and a vacation, even an unscheduled one, so to speak, wouldn't be entirely unwelcome, would it?"

"No," Liz said quietly before Vivian could intervene, "it wasn't unwelcome. In fact, I enjoyed it."

"What did I tell you?" Wheaton said. He drew back to let the waiter place his appetizer in front of him. It was Beluga caviar accompanied by slices of dark Russian bread and a selection of chopped egg, onion, and small green capers. Vivian and Ed had opted for the same;

Liz had declined. She didn't like caviar, and this seemed as good a time as any to stop pretending otherwise.

Wheaton slathered up a slice of bread, took a taste, rolled his eyes in appreciation, and then noticed her empty plate. "None for you, Liz?"

"No, thanks."

"This is great, the best, sixty bucks an ounce. How can you pass it up?"

She shrugged. "Beats me. Look, do you mind if I ask you something?"

"Of course not. Ask me anything. That's what I'm here for."

"What about Tom?"

Wheaton exchanged a quick look with Daugherty. His brow furrowed. "Tom?"

"Tom Wilcox, the anchor for the past five years of this network's nightly news. You do remember him?"

Wheaton's cheeks darkened slightly. "Oh, *Tom*, of course, I just didn't realize at first. What about him?"

"That's what I asked. What happens to him if I come in?"

"Good heavens, Liz," Vivian broke in. "That's hardly something you need to worry about. Wilcox is a big boy."

"He's also been a friend to me. I just want to know what your plans are for him."

Daugherty cleared his throat. The caviar seemed

to have lost its appeal for him. "As to that, Tom has agreed that what he really wants to do is get back into the field. After five years, he's tired of being behind a desk." He caught a warning look from Wheaton and neatly sidestepped. "Which isn't to say that you'd be restricted from doing outside reporting whenever you wished. As Ham has already said, we'd also be looking to showcase you in specials that would give your talent for interviewing plenty of room to stretch."

"Sounds great," Liz murmured. "So Tom's all for this?"

"Absolutely," Wheaton said.

"Down the line," Daugherty agreed.

"There, you see?" Vivian chimed in. "You've got nothing to concern yourself about." She took a forkful of the caviar. "You really should have ordered this. Want some of mine?"

Liz shook her head. She toyed with her water glass, broke a breadstick in two, and listened as the others talked. They were negotiating her future as well as one of the biggest deals in television news history. The numbers being thrown around were breathtaking. She'd made a good salary for several years now, but if she went through with this, she'd be a wealthy woman in no time. And she would, as Vivian had said, have genuine power. World leaders would be only too happy to take her calls, or at least they'd pretend they were. More important from her point of view, she'd have real influence on the news millions of Americans heard each night. She'd be able to help illuminate the mysteries and pitfalls of the rapidly changing world.

"A car and driver available twenty-four hours a day," Wheaton was saying, "as well as the personal hairdresser and a most generous clothing allowance goes without saying."

"Of course," Vivian agreed. She was jotting down notes on the linen tablecloth, heedless of the damage involved. "What about access to the corporate jet? There's really no reason for Liz to fly commercial."

"Sure, sure," Wheaton said. "She'll be on the priority A list."

"Decorating costs for her office?" Vivian asked.

"Twenty thousand per would cover it, don't you think?"

"You're kidding? What, she's supposed to sit on a crate? Thirty."

"Done."

"Which brings us to the subject of how many weeks per year you'd expect her to work," Vivian said. "We all recognize the incredible pressure put on the anchor. She'll need plenty of time to relax and recharge."

"Yes," Wheaton said smoothly, "but we also know Liz is a natural for the job, so the pressure won't be as great on her as it would be on someone without her level of competency. Don't you agree?"

"Possibly, but still I can't help but think that a forty-week maximum would be . . ."

"Impossible. "Forty-eight is the minimum.""

"Forty-two, not a day longer. This woman is going to be a huge star plus lend fantastic credibility to the entire news operation. You're not going to work her into the ground."

"Forty-four," Wheaton said, "and we throw in a personal masseuse to help her work through the stress."

"Hmm, I suppose we can live with that. What do you think, Liz?"

Vivian and Wheaton peered at her expectantly. Daugherty was sitting a little back in his chair with a wary look around his eyes. Of the three, he was the only one who realized something wasn't working.

"Liz?" he asked gently.

She sighed. After a sleepless night alone in her apartment and a morning listening to the three musketeers here plot out her life, it was time she gave them a glimpse of the down side.

"I haven't made up my mind that I want to come back."

Vivian stared at the ceiling. She looked like she was biting the inside of her mouth to keep from laughing.

Wheaton flinched but recovered quickly and

gave her a smile. "Sure, Liz, we understand. You'd rather just give up one of the biggest jobs in America and go back to Virginia."

"Yes," she said softly, "maybe I would."

Wheaton chuckled and even Vivian gave in to a grin, but Daugherty looked serious.

"Wait a minute," he said, "are you on the level with this? You're seriously thinking of getting out of television?"

"Not entirely," Liz admitted. "There's a small station that I—"

"Hold on," Wheaton interjected. "Now look, let's not play games here, all right? We all know why we're here. The network screwed up, we made a mistake and we want Liz back. We're willing to pay a fantastic price to get her. Let's not waste time talking about cute little scenarios that simply aren't going to happen."

"Like my deciding that what I want is actually a whole lot less than what you're offering?" Liz asked mildly. She couldn't muster any anger at Wheaton. It would be like getting angry at a feather pillow. He was all show, no blow, and especially no backbone. Under the veneer of sophistication and professionalism, he was scared to death.

"It wasn't the network who screwed up," she said matter-of-factly, "it was you."

He sputtered and dabbed at his mouth with his napkin. "What are you talking about?"

"Who knew we had a meeting the afternoon my records were stolen? You, me, and Ed here. It was your idea that I put all the files together to show to you—in fact, you insisted on that. Minutes before we were due to meet, when I went to the ladies' room, somebody walked into my office and walked out with the files. Whoever that person was, he knew exactly what he was looking for and where to find it. Doesn't that strike you as odd?"

"Liz . . ." Vivian began. "Think about what you're—"

"Surely you aren't suggesting *I* stole your files?" Wheaton demanded. "That's the most absurd thing I ever heard. Why I—"

"I'm not saying it was you in my office," Liz said. "That was somebody working for Hauster just like it was somebody in his employ who intimidated my witnesses. But he had to know what to take and who to get at. Now maybe you can make a case that it was Ed who told him, but I wouldn't buy it. Ed's willing to cut corners and he puts a premium on keeping his job, but there are limits he won't go beyond. You, on the other hand, strike me as the type who will do anything to get where you think you ought to be."

"I can't believe this," Wheaton said. He had gone pale and there was a little film of sweat on his upper lip. "This is insane. You can't expect me to—"

"Why would he do it?" Daugherty asked. He was looking at Liz closely. "What benefit would there be for him so far as the network was concerned? Or are you suggesting he was more interested in cozying up to Hauster?"

Liz shook her head. She ignored Wheaton's attempt to override her and said, "Remember the leveraged buy-out a few years ago? Most of the financing came from Bank Northeastern, which also happened to hold the serious paper on Hauster. If word got out about his money problems— and it didn't get shot down right away—the bank was liable to take a major loss. Whoever prevented that would be in good with one of this country's biggest financial institutions as well as with the network. Wheaton stood to win all the way around."

"That's crazy!" Wheaton shouted. He shoved his chair back and got to his feet. "I'm out of here. As far as I'm concerned, these negotiations are over."

"Sit down," Daugherty said. His voice was cold as ice.

Wheaton hesitated. There was no reason for him to do as the older man said, but there was something in the way Daugherty looked, so different from his usual manner, that suggested maybe he'd better think about it real seriously.

Slowly, Wheaton sat.

"What?" he demanded.

"You helped Hauster out to stay in good with the money boys? Is that it? You forced me to fire the best correspondent I've ever worked with to save the network's bank the embarrassment of admitting they'd made some bad loans?"

"Some bad loans?" Wheaton repeated. He shook his head in disgust. All pretense at denial dropped away as he sneered. "You're really something, you know that? Sitting in your office day after day thinking you're bringing wisdom and light to the great unwashed. Let me tell you, you're nothing, this network is nothing, without money. Northeastern came through when it was needed. They put the network in the hands of men who know how to run it. Men I respect and I'm not ashamed to serve. It was in everyone's interest to protect deniability on Hauster."

"What the hell does that mean?" Daugherty demanded. He came half out of his seat, glaring at Wheaton. A startled waiter just entering the room with the main part of the meal withdrew hastily.

"Deniability," Ed went on. "What's that? You were protecting Hauster's ass and you were kissing same with the bankers. You little twerp. You don't have the foggiest idea what this network stands for. We're a public trust, for God's sake! Some of us still take that damn seriously."

"Easy," Liz said, putting a hand on his arm. "There's no point getting angry. Hauster's blown,

Northeastern will survive, and the network may end up stronger for all this. Anyway, I think it's likely Wheaton was acting on his own. The higher-ups may not be a bunch of Boy Scouts, but they've got too much sense to risk being tarred with the same brush as Hauster. They would have kept their distance, but Ham here had to get creative.''

"That's true," Daugherty said thoughtfully. He stared at the pale, sweating man across from him, but it was to Liz that he spoke. "What do you suppose we should do about all this?"

Liz took a deep breath. She looked around the table—at Vivian, who was keeping her eyes carefully averted from Wheaton, who had taken on the sick gray color of a man on the edge of collapse, while Daugherty was looking positively exuberent. Softly, she said, "It's what you should do, Ed. I'm out."

Vivian moaned. She put her hands in her face and shook her head slowly back and forth. Liz sighed. She got up, went over to the other women, and gave her a hug. "It's not so bad. You've got plenty of other clients and they're all doing great."

"It was the biggest deal ever." Her gaze was frozen in the thousand-yard stare common to witnesses of catastrophes. "The deal of a lifetime." She looked up, meeting Liz's eyes. Almost silently she mouthed a single word. "Why?"

It was a fair question. Softly, Liz said, "Somebody made me a better offer." She hesitated a fraction of a second before she added, "I just hope it's still on the table."

———— THIRTEEN ————

Deke was mucking out the sheep barn. All things considered, it seemed apt. He felt like what he had in the shovel and there was no point wasting a better chore on the mood he was in.

Maybe Agnes had been right after all. Maybe living alone all these years had made him squirrelly. He hadn't blown his brains out as she so kindly predicted but he *had* made himself doubt that he had any.

What had he been thinking of to let Liz go? She was up in the Big City being wined, dined, and wooed while he was here, feeling like somebody had carved a big hole in him and all the stuff that made life worth living was leaking out of it.

This being in love was even trickier than he'd suspected. He was trying so hard to be noble that it was killing him. What he really wanted was to go up to Washington, D.C., smash a few heads, and drag Liz back home any way he had to. But of course he couldn't because he was too much of a gentleman. He'd stay here, right where he was, and give her the chance to really make up her mind for herself. If she decided against him, those were the breaks. She had every right, it was her life, and whatever she opted for, he'd accept.

He made a disgusted sound deep in his throat and tossed the shovel aside. Outside the barn, he blinked in the sun and tried to settle on something else to do. He was tired, having not slept the night before, but there was no point trying to get any rest, since he'd just toss and turn and drive himself crazy. His stomach was rumbling because he hadn't bothered to eat, but he couldn't muster any interest in putting something together. He could go into town, drop by the diner, but somebody there would be sure to ask where Liz was and he wasn't about to get into a discussion along those lines.

A ride. Yeah, he could do that, a nice, hard ride to make him forget his worries. Except he'd be thinking about going riding with Liz and how good it felt to have her beside him.

He kicked a rock across the yard and rubbed the back of his head. There had to be something. He was a grown man, not some lovestruck kid.

He'd gotten along fine without her for years. Surely he could do so again.

Oh, yeah, right, especially when the mere thought of her was enough to make him hard with yearning. For the first and only time in his life, he wished he'd been born into a different generation, one where men weren't expected to be so all-fired sensitive to the feelings and perogatives of women. It would have made everything a whole lot simpler.

Maybe he'd just head on over to her house and see what he could do about that drainpipe that had come off its braces.

Good thought, Adler. Best place in the world to forget her would be right there in her own house! He was losing it, that was for sure. Next thing, he'd be asking the sheep what they thought he should do.

And all the while, the answer was staring him right in the face. Off by the side of the house the truck squatted, sullen and reluctant, but always amenable to threats of the scrap heap.

Deke walked over and patted it gently. "How'd you like to see the Big City?" he asked.

He could have sworn the engine rumbled, but then it was hard to tell. After all the hours of trying to sell himself on being noble, a refreshing wave of steely determination was washing over him. To hell with fairness and caution and all the rest of it. There came a time when a man had to do what a man had to do.

What Deke did was about eighty mph straight up the highway. He hit the fair streets of Washington, D.C., in under two hours, a new record, and quickly scouted out the big pile of black steel and glass that was the network's headquarters.

Who said it was tough to park in Washington, D.C.? He found a nice spot right out in front. Of course it hadn't been legal to park there for about fifty years, but he didn't let that get in his way. Nobody in their right mind would try towing the truck from hell.

Inside the building on the main floor was the usual setup—banks of elevators, a security desk, a lot of marble and brass. A uniformed security guard took one look at him and approached cautiously.

"Sir?"

"I'm looking for Liz Sherwood," he said. "She's in a meeting here."

The guard gave him one of those steely-eyed looks they learn in security school. He didn't like big guys in rumpled work clothes who came in looking like they were trouble. "That would be Miss Sherwood?"

"For the moment. Got any idea where she is?"

"I couldn't say. If you'd give me your name, I'll call upstairs and—"

"Never mind. I'll find it." He brushed past the

guard and headed for the elevators. Not for nothing had he spent those years down on Wall Street. If memory served, there was only one place meetings like the one Liz was in tended to be held. Under such circumstances, people had an infallible instinct to head for the highest ground.

He pushed the button marked "25" and stood back as the doors closed. The ride was quick and smooth. His ears only popped a little.

The doors opened onto what looked like a private home except it was the lushly furnished reception area for the executive floor. A lushly dressed receptionist was seated behind an inlaid chestnut desk. She looked at him dubiously.

"May I help you, sir?"

"Sure can. Which room is Liz Sherwood in?"

The woman hesitated. She'd been around the television business long enough to know that it had a few quirks. For one thing, you couldn't always tell who was really important and who wasn't. Some of the creative types, the ones who pulled down the biggest bucks, looked like they'd just crawled out from under a rock.

Not that this guy was anything like that. He was flat out gorgeous, even if he was dressed just a little irregularly for the executive floor. Didn't you know somebody like Liz Sherwood would have all the luck.

"She's in the executive dining room," the receptionist said, "but I really don't think they want to be disturbed. It would be better if you—'' She stopped and stared past Deke at the spectacle approaching down the hallway.

That nice Ed Daugherty from news came first. He had his arm around the dark-haired woman in the great suit who looked like she needed the help. But she wasn't anything compared to Wheaton. What in heaven's name had happened to him? He looked like death warmed over.

And where, while the questions were being asked, was Liz Sherwood?

Liz had stopped off in the ladies' room. She needed a few minutes to compose herself. She had no regrets, but the scene with Wheaton had taken a lot out of her. If there'd been a shower available, she would have been tempted to use it, he made her feel that dirty. As it was, she made do with a quick hair brush and a squirt of perfume behind her ears. She'd said her good-byes to Vivian and Ed in the dining room. Any goodbye to Wheaton had seemed superfluous. And she'd promised to stay in touch. Long farewells depressed her. She'd give them a little time to leave and then she'd get on her way.

She was coming out of the ladies' room when she noticed something funny going on in the reception area. Ed and Vivian were still there. Vivian was pounding both her fists in the air, shaking her head and at the same time muttering, ''I knew it, I absolutely knew it. She couldn't level with me, oh, no. She couldn't say there was some man involved. Hmm, *some* man. Now admit it, Ed, this at least makes sense.''

"I wouldn't know,'' Ed said. He smiled pleasantly at Deke and added, ''We left her at the ladies' room. She ought to be along any minute.''

"Appreciate your help,'' Deke said. They seemed like nice enough folks, although when he asked if they happened to know where Liz was, the little lady in the funny suit had given him a look that could have killed.

"Just what makes you such hot stuff?'' she demanded, raking him over from head to toe.

He backed up a foot just to be on the safe side. He'd been away from cities for a while, but it seemed to him that people hadn't been quite that strange when he left. But then he hadn't had much to do with television.

"Now, Viv,'' the guy was saying, ''you don't know that he's responsible for Liz's decision to—''

Just when he was getting interesting, he broke off. Well, he had to, didn't he? Because Liz had caught sight of Deke at the same time he saw her. There they stood, staring at each other like in one of those old-time commercials where the guy and the girl see each other and start running through the grass, sparkling in the sunlight, meeting up in the big happily-ever-after clinch.

Except Deke and Liz didn't run. They walked very deliberately, never taking their eyes off each other. By the time they got up close, they were both looking very serious indeed.

"Well, hi," Liz said.

"I happened to be in the neighborhood and I thought I'd stop by," Deke said.

"What a shame. I was just leaving."

His eyes lightened. Deep within them, hope flared. "Oh, yeah? Where are you going? Maybe I can give you a lift."

"Virginia."

"That far?"

Liz's smile deepened. Her eyes were filled with promise as she nodded. "All the way."

EPILOGUE

Liz opened one eye and peered into another. It was large, brown, and soulful. As she watched, it blinked.

"Get out of here," she muttered, and burrowed deeper into the covers.

The sheep ducked its head regretfully, turned on its tail, and walked off with that regal waddle all sheep seem to have. After a moment or two, Liz could hear it clattering down the stairs.

She sighed and turned over again. Maybe she'd been a little harsh. The sheep was something of a pet, although for the life of her she couldn't figure out how that had happened. True enough, it was the grown-up version of the first lamb she watched being born and it had early on decided that where she went, it went, but there were limits.

She opened both her eyes and glanced hopefully at the other side of the bed, but that only told her what her body had already sensed. The covers were rumpled and a certain familiar warmth clung to them, but Deke himself was already up and about.

Reluctantly, Liz followed. She'd never be a morning person, but she was learning. Besides, she could smell coffee downstairs.

He was standing in the kitchen, having a cup and looking out over the yard toward the orchards. The trees hung heavy with fruit. Picking had started the day before and would continue for several weeks. The crop promised to be bountiful.

He smiled when he saw her and reached for another cup. "Morning. Was that Mary I saw coming down?"

"The one, the only." She gave him a quick kiss and snagged the pot. "I'm getting better, though, don't you think? Sheep in the house don't bother me so long as they behave themselves. Of course, I know I'm still not good with bats."

He laughed, his gaze moving over her tenderly. Disheveled and sleep-flushed, she looked delicious. But then she did every other way, too.

It was a little over a year since that day in Washington, D.C., when Liz and the network parted ways for good. She and Deke had been married almost all that time. The months had gone by so quickly that it almost scared him. Fifty years with her would only be, as the old lawyer joke went, a good start.

Looking at her as she sipped her coffee and did her best to wake up, he thought how nice it would be to take her back to the big four-poster bed upstairs. But duty called and they had to be someplace in a couple of hours. Besides, a little anticipation never hurt.

She saw what he was thinking and shook her head wryly. "We're going to wear out that mattress."

He shrugged, gave her a quick grin, and reached for the door. Over his shoulder he said, "There's always the couch at the office."

She flushed slightly, remembering the workout the couch had gotten just a few days before. When she went upstairs to get dressed, she was smiling.

By the time they finished up the chores, got into the truck, and headed into town, it was midmorning. The day was bright and clear. The flags along Main Street snapped in the breeze.

They had to leave the truck a few blocks from the diner and go the rest of the way on foot. Deke carried the minicam. Crowds were already milling around. A wooden platform had been set up next to the river and decorated with bunting. A piece of red ribbon ran across the opening to the new bridge.

"Not too bad-looking, is it?" Agnes said when she came over to greet them.

"I liked the old one better," Liz said. The new bridge was strictly poured steel and utilitarian in design, lacking the elaborations of the old wrought iron. But it would do the job.

"Bart sorry to be losing his ferry?" she asked.

Agnes hesitated. She glanced at the minicam. "This for the record?"

Liz and Deke exchanged a surreptitious look. Ever since they'd switched WWDY to a heavier concentration on news, including local, people in town were turning media savvy. Just the other day Liz had heard Debbie over at the Pic & Save talking about sound bites. Heaven help them all.

"Not if you don't want it to be," she said matter-of-factly.

Agnes glanced over her shoulder, assured herself nobody else was listening, and said, "He's taking it downriver to Branford. Got a license to start up there. And he's talking about branching out to other parts. Can you imagine that? Gonna turn himself into some kind of transportation mogul."

"Wouldn't put it past him," Liz said. "Pretty soon from one end of the country to the other it'll be Woodsley diners and ferrys. You won't be able to go anywhere without tripping over them."

"That's what I thought," Agnes said. She moved off, shaking her head.

Truth be told, Bart wasn't looking too unhappy for a man who was seeing a tidy little business being made obsolete. But then he did have several hundreds folks on hand to sell sandwiches and drinks to.

Around about noon, the dignitaries from the state capital got up and made a few speeches. Deke filmed that while Liz circulated in the crowd, getting people's reactions. The first car was driven across with Grannie Georgette Eugenia Winston Woodsley, the oldest resident of Woodsley, in the front seat. Everybody cheered and the band struck up "Camptown Races" for some reason nobody knew.

With the ceremonies concluded, the celebration began. On the stretch of riverbank where a plaque was set up to commemorate the arrival of the first Woodsleys in the area, people gathered for the traditional apple pie contest held every time a bridge was opened over the Maupeechuk.

"Had one the last time, too," Grannie Georgette told everyone. "Back in '01 when the old bridge was finished." She shook her head regretfully. "Nobody would have thought it'd be done and gone this soon. Don't make things like they used to." She went off to get another cup of cider and judge the sack contest.

Deke and Liz stayed until the party started to wind down in late afternoon. Then they headed over to WWDY to do the evening broadcast. Liz laughed when she saw one of the items on the wire.

"You've got to see this," she said when she took it to Deke.

He glanced at it and shook his head in amazement. "What goes around comes around."

The item said: "Ron Hauster, the failed tycoon whose bankruptcy last year sent shock waves through financial markets, has announced the repurchase of his flagship casino in Baton Rouge. Sources believe Hauster secured the deal with financing from off-shore contacts. Mr. Hauster was quoted as saying, 'I'm on the comeback trail. It's the American way.' Named to head the casino management is former television industry executive, Hamilton Wheaton."

Liz was tempted to lead with the story, but she played it straight and gave it thirty seconds when they were ten minutes into the broadcast. So far as Woodsley went, that was all it merited. However, as she'd expected, the nightly network news played it differently.

"Tom's looking good," she said as she and Deke settled in the office to catch the network feed. They were, for a change, sitting on the couch, feet propped up on the coffee table, companionably cozy.

"Ought to with that new contract," Deke said.

After Liz bowed out of the anchor slot, the network had decided Tom Wilcox wasn't so bad after all. They'd had cause to reconsider that when they confronted his new agent. Vivian hadn't wasted any time. She'd convinced Tom he hadn't been getting a fair deal—no job security for one thing—but she was just the person to fix that.

Ed Daugherty still bore the scars from that negotiation, but he didn't mind too much. The ratings were up, the big boys were off his back, and Tom's Q was through the ceiling. Something about the public liking him better since he gained ten pounds and let his hair go gray around the edges.

"Will you look at that," Liz said. Tom had film of Ham Wheaton at the newly repurchased casino. The pinstriped suit and school tie were gone. He was wearing a shiny gray suit, very padded at the shoulders, his hair was longer, and he had sunglasses on. There were a couple of showgirls behind him and a burly fellow nearby who appeared to be his bodyguard. In addition, Ham seemed to have acquired a Brooklyn accent.

Tom played it straight, which Liz admired, but he was smiling as he signed off. The world had managed to get through another day more or less intact. The apples were ripening, the breeze was stirring, and the sheep were doing whatever it was sheep did.

One of these days, Liz thought, she was going to replace the couch. But in the meantime, they might as well get some use out of it.

Deke thought so, too. He drew her to him, his mouth warm against her skin. The passion built as it always did, hot and sweet, taking them into a world that would forever be their own.

SHARE THE FUN . . .
SHARE YOUR NEW-FOUND TREASURE!!

You don't want to let your new books out of your sight? That's okay. Your friends can get their own. Order below.

No. 1 ALWAYS by Catherine Sellers
A modern day "knight in shining armor." Forever . . . for always!

No. 2 NO HIDING PLACE by Brooke Sinclair
Pretty government agent & handsome professor = mystery & romance.

No. 3 SOUTHERN HOSPITALITY by Sally Falcon
North meets South. War is declared. Both sides win!!!

No. 4 WINTERFIRE by Lois Faye Dyer
Beautiful NY model and rugged Idaho rancher find their own magic.

No. 5 A LITTLE INCONVENIENCE by Judy Christenberry
Liz faces every obstacle Jason throws at her—even his love.

No. 6 CHANGE OF PACE by Sharon Brondos
Can Sam protect himself from Deirdre, the green-eyed temptress?

No. 7 SILENT ENCHANTMENT by Lacey Dancer
Was she real? She was Alex's true-to-life fairy tale princess.

No. 8 STORM WARNING by Kathryn Brocato
Passion raged out of their control—and there was no warning!

No. 9 PRODIGAL LOVER by Margo Gregg
Bryan is a mystery. Could he be Keely's presumed dead husband?

No. 10 FULL STEAM by Cassie Miles
Jonathan's a dreamer—Darcy is practical. An unlikely combo!

No. 11 BY THE BOOK by Christine Dorsey
Charlotte and Mac give parent-teacher conference a new meaning.

No. 12 BORN TO BE WILD by Kris Cassidy
Jenny shouldn't get close to Garrett. He'll leave too, won't he?

No. 13 SIEGE OF THE HEART by Sheryl McDanel Munson
Nick pursues Court while she wrestles with her heart and mind.

No. 14 TWO FOR ONE by Phyllis Herrmann
What is it about Cal and Elliot that has Leslie seeing double?

No. 15 A MATTER OF TIME by Ann Bullard
Does Josh *really* want Christine or is there something else?

No. 16 FACE TO FACE by Shirley Faye
Christi's definitely not Damon's type. So, what's the attraction?

No. 17 OPENING ACT by Ann Patrick
Big city playwright meets small town sheriff and life heats up.

No. 18 RAINBOW WISHES by Jacqueline Case
Mason is looking for more from life. Evie may be his pot of gold!

No. 19 SUNDAY DRIVER by Valerie Kane
Carrie breaks through all Cam's defenses showing him how to love.

No. 20 CHEATED HEARTS by Karen Lawton Barrett
T.C. and Lucas find their way back into each other's hearts.

No. 21 THAT JAMES BOY by Lois Faye Dyer
Jesse believes in love at first sight. Will he convince Sarah?

No. 22 NEVER LET GO by Laura Phillips
Ryan has a big dilemma. Kelly is the answer to *all* his prayers.

No. 23 A PERFECT MATCH by Susan Combs
Ross can keep Emily safe but can he save himself from Emily?

No. 24 REMEMBER MY LOVE by Pamela Macaluso
Will Max ever remember the special love he and Deanna shared?

Meteor Publishing Corporation
Dept. 392, P. O. Box 41820, Philadelphia, PA 19101-9828

Please send the books I've indicated below. Check or money order only—no cash, stamps or C.O.D.s (PA residents, add 6% sales tax). I am enclosing $2.95 plus 75¢ handling fee for *each* book ordered.

Total Amount Enclosed: $_____.

_____ No. 1	_____ No. 7	_____ No. 13	_____ No. 19
_____ No. 2	_____ No. 8	_____ No. 14	_____ No. 20
_____ No. 3	_____ No. 9	_____ No. 15	_____ No. 21
_____ No. 4	_____ No. 10	_____ No. 16	_____ No. 22
_____ No. 5	_____ No. 11	_____ No. 17	_____ No. 23
_____ No. 6	_____ No. 12	_____ No. 18	_____ No. 24

Please Print:
Name _____/
Address _____ Apt. No. _____
City/State _____ Zip _____

Allow four to six weeks for delivery. Quantities limited.